A LITTLE WICKED

JANET R. MACREERY

outskirtspress

DENVER, COLORADO

Outskirts Press, Inc.
http://www.outskirtspress.com

ISBN: 978-1-4787-3346-1

Library of Congress Control Number: 2014906223

Outskirts Press and the "OP" logo are trademarks belonging to Outskirts Press, Inc.

PRINTED IN THE UNITED STATES OF AMERICA

for my ancestors

Chapter One

My own coughing woke me. One moment, I slept, snuggled under my scratchy, woolen plaid. The next I was amid a whirl of blankets with the bitter stench of gunpowder and smoke flung about me. The beasts made frightful moans. Mother ordered me into my boots and pushed me through the door of our stone bothie into the freezing darkness, the fires and gun blasts to our backs. Screams, cries, bellows and choked begs trailed us on the howling wind as we hustled down the glen toward the hillock where I used to play brave heart with Gilbert and the Henderson lads.

"What is happening?" I asked.

"Quiet, Dory," Mother said. "They will find us."

"Who?"

"Campbells."

The Campbells were attacking us? The mention of that clan should stir a flash of anger but this time I felt fear. Pure life-threatening fear.

The Campbells had been staying in Glencoe for two weeks. They came to collect the king's taxes. Their Captain, Robert Campbell of Glenlyon also claimed to be visiting his niece, who happened to be my mother. On what cause would he kill his own kin?

I looked to Mother for answers but she stared stone silent at my father, the second son to the chief of our small clan. We were the MacDonalds of Glencoe led by my grandfather, the MacIain.

The horrible sounds of the killings reached us. Agonizing screams of people and beasts as bullets and blades ripped them from life. The dozen people hiding with us sat with eyes frightened wide or shut tight against the horror. We clamped our hands over our mouths to stifle cries. Breath, warm for an instant than ice cold, puffed onto my freezing fingers as I covered my own mouth.

Father motioned for us to lie flat on our stomachs. We shielded ourselves with the tartan plaids, other blankets and then tree limbs. The more we blended with the ground, the harder it would be for the king's Redcoats to see us. Had it been spring or summer, we could have hidden in the high grasses, now held down by snow. As soon as we were laying behind what little protection the hillock provided, Father turned to Mother.

"I have to find John," he whispered. The pained look in Mother's eyes begged him not to go and in the same moment conveyed she knew his duty to his brother, to our clan. Father broke eye contact with Mother and ran back to the murderous scene.

The morning sun cracked above the horizon showing us little more than wind-driven snow, flashes of fire and dense smoke. It was not the first time I had been belly down on the ground covered in tree branches, trying to breathe shallow, yet enough to stay alive. I had been on raids with the lads, reclaiming cattle that had been spirited away from our herds. Roaming the beautiful fields, scaling the steep path to Coire Gabhail, and scurrying through the mountains freed me from the closed in chores in the bothie. The sweet air filled my lungs and lifted my heart. Mother knew I went on the raids but pretended not to. She did not think cattle rustling a proper way for a lass like me to spend time, even though it ran in our blood on her side of the family, too. She preferred me to cook, sew, scrub, and go on skylark hunts with Merlin.

Merlin! Oh no, poor Merlin! Trapped in his cage in our now in-cinerated house. Common soldiers were too dense to know the value of a beautiful bird of prey like my Merlin. They would think my bird useless and let him die in the flames.

My heart broke and fell to ashes that the wind mixed with those of our baile and blew away.

Black smoke thicker than morning fog crept, pricking and poking, into my lungs making it near impossible to keep from coughing. I pushed air through my nose to force out the smells of the burning peat, sod and thatch from our roofs as well as the burning flesh from our animals and clan members. Slimy, sticky phlegm coated my throat. My eyes teared from smoke and, had I still had my heart, from anger and sadness.

Campbells scouted the area outside our baile looking for more MacDonalds to kill. I dared not move but squeezed my throat shut so I would not cough for fear of alerting the enemy to our hiding spot.

The scorching fires obliterated buildings, food stocks and animals as our people continued to flee. Snow melted under my body and soaked into my clothes. Grateful to have on my warmest stockings, I found it strange that father had told me to wear them to bed that night. The snowstorm had been raging for hours but our house had been comfortable enough. The black cattle and wee sheep slept inside with us in a small pen and they always gave off a good amount of heat. Father had also left the cash sack next to a bag of oats, not behind the loose stone in the hearth. Mother had been able to grab both bags during our escape.

If Father had a darna shealladh, if he had seen what could happen, would he not have attacked the Campbells first? After a true second sight warning, he would have stopped the attack, not prepared us to run. Perhaps Father had not had a vision. Since the time Glenlyon and his men arrived, Mother and Father had been whispering to each other and exchanging strange looks. Had they feared an attack all along? How did they know it was coming and when?

My body jolted with an involuntary cough. Too late, I covered my mouth with the corner of a blanket. Mother grabbed my arm. Footsteps. Rushing toward us. Boots crunched on snow as the wind howled. The footsteps stopped so near to where we lay in the snow, I could hear the hard breathing of a man.

Moments later, he came over the top of the hillock. I was gripped by fear, sure I was about to meet my ancestors. An instant passed. I sat face to face with my uncle, John.

"Maclain is dead," he said. "We have to move on."

Chapter Two

"We must go back, sir," young Ian Henderson said, "help the wounded, gather what food is left and avenge our chief."

Avenge our chief. My grandfather.

"There are no wounded," John told us. "Glenlyon's men finish their kills. They are right now looting our bothies and burning anything too heavy to carry. I heard them speaking of reinforcements on the way down the Devil's Staircase. We have to survive, get word to the king of this atrocity and plead for our legal property back."

"Alasdair?" Mother asked.

"I sent him to the river banks to check for survivors."

Mother nodded, but said nothing further.

With MacIain dead, John, his oldest son, was now the 13th Chief of Clan MacDonald of Glencoe. The naming of a new chief is destined to be a sad day as it is always the day of death of the old chief. While we all knew he would one day die, we hoped it would be in battle or from old age. No one could have expected MacIain's death to be this tragic. Men, Scotsmen, who had accepted our Highland hospitality for a fortnight, had murdered my grandfather as he woke from sleep. Shameful. There was no honor in it.

The sun gained height in the sky and soon the scavenging murderers would know our position. We had to leave the glen, our home, and hide.

"We will go south," John, the new chief told us. "Shelter is our first priority."

"Who will take us in?" Mother asked. "There's no way to know who has sided with the Campbells. Anyone could be our enemy."

"Almost anyone," John said. "The Stewarts of Appin will shelter us. They put their hatred of the Campbells above all else, even their hatred of King William of Orange. We will not have to hide for long. Glenlyon's men have no stomach to meet in a fair fight. They will burn our homes, then flee and stay gone."

The new chief had spoken. No one reminded him how far Appin was or that there must be scores more MacDonalds out in the furious storm. What would happen to them? Would they be able to find us?

Did my father know where to find us?

We snuck away from the hillock, two and three people at a time to hide behind an outcropping of large rocks. We then snuck behind a larger hill. The snow slowed a bit, allowing us to see where we were going. The wind felt no less icy. I wondered why my tears did not freeze on my face.

We tripped and slipped on the hillsides at a quick pace. Traveling in small clumps, we huddled together to fight the wind, wrapped in our plaids and blankets. Campbells skulked about and could chase if they saw us through the snow. Our first goal was to reach the opposite side of Meall Mor. On the southwest side of that big hill stood a small forest. The trees would provide some shelter from the wind, hiding places and firewood.

The hills and mountains of Glencoe were steep and overlapped each other, running in ridges. The landscape was foreboding and beautiful at the same time. Truly awesome. Visitors to the glen thought those of us who lived here took the breathtaking sights for granted. What they did not know was we understood how dangerous the glen could be. When we trekked through the glen, Gilbert and I pretended we were sneaking along the backs of sleeping dragons. Now, with the fires and smoke billowing along with the storm, it seemed the dragons were waking.

Most of my mind concentrated on where to put my next footstep but part of me tried to figure out what happened. Who knew about it? Why did they launch such a heinous attack? What would happen next?

I had no answers. My memory carried me back to the day when the king's Redcoats had first arrived in our baile.

Gilbert and I had taken Merlin vole hunting by the River Coe. We arrived back to see the MacIain waiting in front of his bothie. His two sons John, the first-born and Alasdair, my father, stood beside him with dignity and pride. All three wore the clan's tartan in trews form for added protection for their legs against a cold day. They wore jackets made of wool, their swords and dirk handles evident for all to see. The MacIain was an imposing man. His loyalty to the clan's way of life was absolute even if it put him at odds with the government. It was what I loved most about him. He made concessions only when the survival of the clan depended on it. His education had been complete, learning languages and customs in the courts of several countries, but his warrior heart ruled his actions.

"The last scout report came from Inverlochy," Father had said. "They'll be here soon."

MacDonald clan scouts had told of the advancing company hours before we could see them. Our three men waited as the King's men approached. It was an awkward meeting.

"Alasdair," Glenlyon said with a nod. MacIain returned the nod but not the greeting. The two men seemed about the same age, which made Glenlyon a little old to be marching through the Highlands in February on someone else's orders. His reduced status due in part to cattle raids on his lands. Some of those raids carried out by our own lads.

"What's your business here, Glenlyon?" MacIain said after a short silence. Merlin chose that moment to pull on his ties by flapping his wings with all his might. It lasted a few seconds but felt like hours as my muscles strained to keep my gloved hand and arm unmoving. None of the MacDonalds turned to look at us. Merlin often misbehaved.

"It's the crown's business, Alasdair, not mine or the Campbells'," he replied. "The towns are overflowing with people. My men need housing and provisions."

MacIain stood silent again for a few moments. Everyone present knew he would allow Glenlyon's men to live among us, eat our food and enjoy our fires because that was the Highland way. We were proud of many things, how we treated outsiders was one of them.

"This is bad," Gilbert whispered. "Glenlyon must blame us for his bitter losses."

"I doubt he would stay with us if he had any other choice," I whispered back. "It is a terrible cold winter and his men need shelter and food. He is just making the best of things."

"Sometimes you remind me you are a young lass of only twelve years."

I took the insult with a silent glower. If I allowed myself a greater reaction, we would have disturbed the negotiation, again.

"Of course," Glenlyon added after the silence had stretched on, "it is an opportunity to spend time with my niece." This comment meant to close the deal. Glenlyon's niece, my mother, was married to MacIain's younger son, my father, making the two men family, distant family. In the glen, family is family.

"It will take some time to get everyone settled," MacIain said. The two men started giving orders. In an instant, the baile had become active. Distrust hung thick in the air as the Campbell and MacDonald men followed the orders of their leaders, no matter how much they did not want to perform their tasks.

My foot slipped on a patch of snow and brought my mind to the present. I realized how cold my ears were and lifted my plaid to cover my head. Of course, then my backside got cold.

Meall Mor grew larger to our west and Glencoe fell further behind us. Perhaps if my heart had not been shattered and carried away on the wind after I realized Merlin had to be dead, I would have been mourning my clansmen, my family and my grandfather. I did not know the fate of many others including my father, including Gilbert.

However, I could not think about those things. The hole where my heart used to be could not think of the missing and the dead. It had to move forward.

Chapter Three

My mind was too busy to want food or drink but my body disagreed. My stomach grumbled and my throat felt dry. I could see the tips of the trees but knew it would be a while before we stopped. I unwrapped my right hand from the blanket and snatched a bit of snow from the ground. It melted in my mouth and eased the strain in my throat, at least for a moment.

Winter sunlight was rare in the glen. For the short time the sun was in the sky, clouds covered it. We trudged toward our goal. The only sounds, the constant coughing common to our people. It took hours of hard work to get to our hiding place in the woods and once we arrived, there was no time to rest. There was plenty to do and not much time before the sun set again sinking us into frigid darkness.

"We need a fire," John said. It was the first I had heard him or anyone else speak since we set out around Meall Mor. "We will freeze to our deaths if we don't have heat."

"One large fire, sir?" Ian asked. "Or several smaller ones?"

"One," John said without hesitation. "It will have to do. Get moving."

"Aye, sir." Ian and Roderick mumbled in unison.

John turned to me. "Dory, find some rocks. If you cannae pick it up, it is too big."

"How many, sir?" I asked.

"One rock for each person here. Get a few more in case others find us. Quick, quick, before the sun is gone."

Searching the ground, I tried not to think about the 'others' who might find us. Why John wanted me to find rocks escaped me but I did not question it. Everyone busied themselves with tasks. Some prepared an area to build the fire. Others broke branches and gathered smaller twigs to feed the fire once it got started. Larger limbs were gathered and leaned against standing trees, bracing limbs against each other to keep the wind from taking them. Under these little shelters, others cleared snow, leaves and pine needles aside and placed smaller tree branches on the ground. When not taking a shift as guard, these shelters would serve as protection from the wind and as beds for those who could sleep.

I wondered why John had not assigned anyone to hunt for rabbit for our dinner or look for an unfrozen burn for water. Perhaps he thought it too dangerous to stray from the group.

It did not take long to find the first four rocks. I put them next to the woodpile. On my next trip back with more rocks, I saw Ian and his brother Roderick slamming a piece of flint against the steel blade of a sword. Sparks jumped in the air but did not quite reach the small pile of kindling set at the tip of the blade.

"Lower, you addle-brain," Roderick scolded. "We'll be frozen through before you can light that fire."

"You're the one who made a wee pile of leaves."

"That's all you need if you know what you're doing."

"An expert are you? Then you do it!" Ian said. "I'm sick of you always telling me what to do. Just 'cause you're older don't make you wiser. Just means you'll die sooner."

"You will both die by my sword if I don't see a fire soon," John said.

I had been dealing with the Henderson lads for years and knew neither one would admit he was wrong. If we were going to have a fire, I would have to help. Instead of picking up another rock, I scooped up more leaves and wee twigs and walked over to the lads. I dumped the high pile of kindling at the point of the sword without a word. Then I returned to my rock search. Ian bent over the sword again and struck the blade closer to the tip. Smoke spewed from the effort and the kindling started to glow. Ian blew until the glow got bigger. Roderick added twigs and the small flames crackled as they devoured the wood offerings. Soon the fire grew large enough to add branches.

I glanced up at the growing flames with true yearning but returned to my task. My feet, which I had not been able to feel for hours, stung from the cold. I wrapped my plaid tighter around my body and searched for more rocks. It took a half hour to find another six rocks. With one left to find, I was anxious to be finished and stand by the fire. The crackling sounds made the ache to be warm greater. There were no more good-sized rocks nearby and I was cold and tired. I picked up a smaller rock.

"Good enough," I muttered as I placed it on the pile.

John looked unhappy. "By the fire," he said.

Relief at getting warm overruled any shame I might have felt for a not completing my task to the best of my ability. I stepped over to the fire and put my hands as close to the flame as I could.

"Dory!" John yelled.

Startled, I almost jumped into the flames. What? Why was he so cross? He told me to stand by the fire.

"The rocks, Dory," he said. "Put the rocks on the edge of the fire. We need them hot before we can use them."

I wondered if being chief had already driven him mad. But what did I care if he wanted hot rocks? It meant I could be close to the fire. I did as I was told and carried the rocks, a few at a time, close enough to the flames to heat them.

Other people had jobs by the fire, too. Ian and Roderick were poking it, trying to get every piece of bark to burn in order to make the wood we had last all night. Delicious smells wafted from a pan where a few women mixed water and oats.

Oats? Water? Pan? Where did all of it come from? I remembered Mother grabbing our oat bag on the way out the door. Had other people grabbed flasks of water and pans? How did they know to have something ready?

Once all the rocks were in place, I squatted next to Mother as she helped make oatmeal. I did not want to give John the chance to yell at me again. Besides, I was close enough to the fire to feel its heat. My fingers and face hurt as they warmed. I should have been relieved. I had heat, the smell of food and my mother. But I had many questions.

"Where did all the food come from, Mother?"

"Suspicion," she said her face slick with sweat. "Glenlyon is a devious man, trying to eat us out of house and home and then murder us as we slept. Look at the state he has forced us into, all the people he has hurt, using my family connection to do it. A little wicked goes a long, way. Remember that, Dory. We have food tonight, wee one, because MacDonalds are kind enough to take in our enemy but smart enough not to trust them."

The hot steam swirling off the oatmeal was almost as satisfying as the few bites I had. Heat was the most important thing. Food second. I tried not to think about how much better oatmeal tasted with a little honey from Gilbert's bees. We ate our tiny meal in silence, instead of the rousing storytelling we had around the night fires in the glen.

"Ian and Roderick, get some sleep," John said. "I will take the first shift of guard duty."

Without comment, the brothers got up from the fire and headed to the closest shelter.

"Rocks," John said. "You'll be wanting a rock to hold while you sleep."

I gathered all those rocks so we could hold them while we slept? Ian gave Roderick a confused look but each lad chose a rock I had put by the fire and disappeared beyond the branches of a shelter.

"I'll wake you when I get them up, Dory," John said. He turned to Mother. "Those two cannae be guards by themselves. They would let the entire Redcoat Army sneak in while they fought with each other over who was more observant. Dory will help them stay on task."

The few other lasses my age in the glen were happy to spend their time sewing, cooking and scrubbing. I would rather be by the burn and out with Merlin hunting voles. Being a guard for the group was a natural fit for me.

"I'll get up with them," Mother said.

"No need. Dory can handle it. Besides, when Alasdair gets here, he will be furious if you are not well rested."

Mother gave John a strange look and opened her mouth to say something when she began to cough, the kind of cough that does not seem to stop.

Chapter Four

It turned out John had not gone mad when he ordered me to gather rocks and put them near the fire. In fact, he proved to be wise. Holding a hot rock against my belly and wrapping my arms around it was the only way I got any rest. Mother and I slept wrapped together in both our plaids and the extra blanket. Sometime before our guard shift, I woke with chattering teeth and realized my rock had cooled. Mother and I went back to the fire to reheat our sleeping rocks and ourselves several times in the night. The flames snapped and crackled against the freezing night air. Every guard duty shift, even mine with the Hendersons, had company as people had to come back to the fire after waking with cold rocks.

Whenever I got up, I searched the camp to see if anyone new had found us. Twice there were one or two new people. Not the ones I was looking for. Not my father. Not Gilbert. Not yet.

I tried not to worry about it. John hoped he would be leading us back in a day or so. Father would be able to fend for himself with no problem in that short amount of time. He was a Glencoe MacDonald, strong and brave. I worried about the others he would be obliged to help and whether they might slow his progress. Father would figure it out.

When our rocks were warm again, Mother and I went back to our tree.

Too soon, the sun came up. It would have been more welcome had it brought any heat. No one looked well rested and two people burned themselves on the oatmeal pan. Again, when the small portion of the clan gathered around the fire it was not to listen to the seannachie tell a tale of past glory. We waited for instructions on what would happen next.

"I will go to Appin and find some Stewarts," John said. "I'll get what supplies I can. Ian and Roderick, go north and west. Travel one day, camp where you can and return the next day. Take note of everything you see and do not let anyone see you. Everyone else stay here. Others may find our camp."

"You'll leave weapons so we may defend ourselves," Mother said. Even though the fire was not that strong, her face reddened and she seemed to be sweating. "In case it is not Glencoe MacDonalds that find us."

"There are not many to spare."

"Weapons or MacDonalds?"

John hesitated. Mother was pushing her luck with the new chief, even if she was his sister-in-law. She should have been showing him respect instead of questioning his leadership. It would have been within his rights to punish her with a slap. Without another word, he brushed a pile of pine needles aside revealing a few small swords, daggers and a dirk. He covered them again and headed south out of camp.

I wondered if Mother had questioned John because she was upset Father had not shown, yet. I was.

Part of me wished John had sent me with the Henderson lads but scouting was tricky. The smaller the group the easier it was to move about. Besides, if I stayed at camp, I might see Father.

There were few chores to do in camp as we waited but somehow people found ways to keep busy. Mother and some of the women had gathered the foodstuffs together and were trying to figure out how to ration it. We did not know how many days we would be away from the baile or if there would be any food there when we returned. Some of the men began using whatever they could find on the forest floor to build rabbit traps to add to the food supply. The thought of rabbit meat made my belly gurgle.

Less than an hour after John left, rustling sounds came from the opposite direction. Those of us left in camp stood still and stopped breathing. At least, I stopped breathing. John had been exploring the vast areas around the glen since boyhood and knew his way around the area well. It could not be him.

"Ian?" Mother called. It was much more probable the Henderson lads had gotten turned around and wound up wandering back on us from the wrong side. Another reason John should have sent me with them. "That you, Roderick?"

No one answered. The rustling got louder.

Mother stepped over to the pile of pine needles and grabbed a dagger. Others followed, including me. I grabbed a sword and held the hilt with two hands. Part of me expected her to object but she did not. It should have made me proud, instead it frightened me.

Abraham, the oldest of the group stood, sword in hand.

"Tell us yer name so we can tell yer family what became of yeh!" he yelled.

More people grabbed weapons, some from the pine needle pile, but most appeared from folds in clothing. Salty liquid pooled in the corners of my mouth.

"State yer name!" Abraham yelled.

"Alasdair MacIain of the Glencoe MacDonalds!" a voice called back. "I have three others with me!"

Father! Father had found us. I dropped my sword and ran toward the voice.

"Wait, lassie!" Abraham called. "It could be a trick!"

It took all I had to stop running and wait. A few seconds later, Father appeared in the clearing. It was him. I wanted to hug him as I had as a child but there was something in his arms. Someone, actually. It was Gilbert's mother. He guided her, more like half carried her, as they walked. She was dragging her feet, looking off to the side and muttering. I looked around the small group but did not see Gilbert.

Everyone in camp started moving again, throwing blankets around the newcomers, coaxing the small flames and returning weapons to their hiding spots. I kept glancing at Gilbert's mother. After the new-comers settled in front of the fire, Father told us of the tragedies he had seen since he left us behind the hillock.

"Our homes are burned, our animals stolen or slaughtered. Our journey led us through more horrors. MacDonalds who had escaped the Campbell weapons only to die in flight. Frozen en route. When we passed old man Herman's body, his own footsteps surrounded his corpse. He must have lost his way in the swirl of the snow and collapsed."

When I could not wait another moment, I knelt next to Gilbert's mother.

"Where's Gilbert?" I asked.

"Dory," Mother whispered. "Hush. Cannae you see?"

"See what?" I asked.

"My boy," Gilbert's mother said in a quiet voice. "M-m-my boy."

"No, I don't see him."

She looked up at me with the big confused eyes of a child. "Who?"

"Gilbert. Where is Gilbert?"

"He saw the bean nighe."

Everyone in camp stopped what they were doing and stared at her.

"He came back from the burn with water for the morning and said he saw the bean nighe. His father called him feeble and told him to feed the animals. My lad was sure. He saw her washing the blood out of a kilt. It looked like his own kilt, the one he was wearing."

She mumbled on for a while. I tried to understand what she was telling us. A bean nighe is a fairy of death. Seeing an old washerwoman getting blood out of clothes was a sign that the person who saw the fairy would die in battle the next day. If Gilbert was right, if he had seen a bean nighe, that meant he had to be dead. Killed by Glenlyon's men.

A hand landed hard on my arm and I jumped. Gilbert's mother looked me in the eyes.

"Gone. The bean nighe took my Gilbert."

Without my heart, my mind could not keep up with all the sadness. Gilbert was dead? Kind, generous, Gilbert gone? How could that be?

Death was a regular occurrence in the glen but when someone's child died, no one knew what to say and sort of ignored the mother. After an hour of muttering to herself, Gilbert's mother took the smallest of the rocks I had gathered and laid down in one of the shelters.

We spent the rest of the daylight hours gathering firewood, making small meals and keeping the rocks hot. I spent the last quarter hour before sunset looking for more rocks, larger ones and thinking about Gilbert.

"A peregrine falcon would be faster and more beautiful, of course," Gilbert had told me the day he gave me my Merlin.

Not to me. Merlin was the most beautiful bird I had ever seen, even for a common buzzard. Brown feathers covered his head, back, tail, chest, and legs. Feathers on his throat, belly and the undersides of his tail and wings were the color of fresh cream and a spot of black tipped his yellow beak. An obstinate attitude glinted in his dark brown eyes. Gilbert had caught Merlin in a field and, with his father's help, trained him by my next birthday.

Gilbert gave me a glove to protect my hand and forearm from Merlin's sharp talons, too. We often went out to the fields and practiced calling him to my glove. An offering of a small dead mouse on the glove helped us get Merlin to do what we wanted.

A fancy lord came through Glencoe with his peregrine falcon about a year after Gilbert trained Merlin. The falcon had a light blue leather hood with a small tassel sticking straight out the top. Gilbert said the expensive hood covered the bird's eyes in order to keep the bird calm. Merlin always stayed calm. I wanted to have a contest with the two birds but Gilbert warned me not to. If Merlin won, the rich lord could make trouble for the clan. That did not mean Gilbert thought Merlin would win, but he thought Merlin might.

"Alasdair," Mother said, interrupting my thoughts. "It's been a while since Evelyn went to rest. I should check on her. Perhaps a taste of oatmeal will make her feel a bit better."

Mother was not gone long when Father told me to bring the mead jug after her.

"Mother," I called from outside the shelter. "Father sent me with the jug."

When she did not answer, I ducked under the large limbs. Mother cradled Gilbert's mother in her arms, rocking her like a baby and singing an old mourning tune. The pale blue skin of my friend's mother and the grief and sorrow in my own mother's voice told me all I needed to know. Every member of Gilbert's family was now dead.

If I had still had a heart, surely that would have broken it.

Chapter Five

A few of the men disappeared with her body and returned, sweating and shivering a while later. I stared at the small rock Gilbert's mother had used the whole time they were gone. After the men returned, I went back to work looking for more rocks, the largest ones I could lift. No one else would die from the cold because of a small rock. That night when it was my turn to sleep, I took the smallest rock myself. John had returned by the third time I got up to reheat my rock during the night. He looked tired and concerned but determined.

At sunup, Father and John talked away from the group in low tones. I hoped this meant we would be going home. The glen would not be the same without my best friend, Gilbert, but it was our home.

After a morning meal, which included some dried hare John had gotten from an Appin Stewart, John stood.

"It is almost time to go back. From what I have learned, Glenlyon's men are gone and show no interest in returning. Some of our people have already begun the work ahead. I heard many disturbing rumors on my short journey. We need to find out the truth and we cannae do that from a camp in the woods. We leave to rebuild our baile tomorrow morning."

One more day in the woods. I could handle that knowing the follow day would return us to the glen. Besides, I was one of the lucky ones who had my family together. We set about our chores, readying packs for easier carrying. Mother and I worked together as we often did at home. We barely spoke, other than her instructions to me, but we did not work in silence. Mother's constant cough turned into more of a hacking. She started wincing and her spit seemed dark, almost black. We took turns napping as well as getting chores done.

John wanted everyone rested for the journey. We had already lost too many people to freezing conditions, sickness and starvation as well as the murdering Campbells.

The Henderson lads returned at suppertime with another lad our age.

"Calum!" I said. "You're alive!" I winced at the amount of surprise in my voice.

"Barely," Roderick said with a mocking laugh. "We found him hiding in the low bushes by a frozen burn. He almost ran when he saw us until Ian yelled out his name. I think he pissed his trews."

I could not help it. I looked at his legs. The material surrounded them looked dry to me. Calum blushed anyway. The three lads came closer to the fire. Calum stared at the oatmeal heating in the pan in Mother's hand.

"Have you eaten, lad?" John asked.

"We gave him some oats and water out of our packs when we found him," Ian bragged.

"And not a morsel since," Calum muttered.

"Come, rest up, lads. We leave in the morning."

"Leave for where?" Ian asked.

"Home," I said. Concern slipping into my mind. Where else would we go?

"May we give you our report, sir," Roderick said to John.

"Certainly."

Ian and Roderick looked at each other. Calum looked around at the trees. He seemed to be searching for something specific.

"Perhaps we should speak with you in private, sir?" Ian asked.

"Tell me what you heard," John replied and put a spoonful of oatmeal in his mouth.

"It's about the attack, sir," Roderick said. "It wasn't Glenlyon."

"What are you saying child?" Abraham asked. "My eyes may be old but they recognize my enemy when they see him."

"It was carried out by Glenlyon but ordered by…by…"

"The king." All eyes turned to John at the sound of his voice. "I heard that same rumor in Appin. I was hoping it wasn't true."

"We think it is, sir," Roderick continued. "We heard it from more than one source. Overheard it. Men talking around campfires and while tending their animals. It was punishment for MacIain being late to swear loyalty to King William and Queen Mary."

"That is an excuse," John said. "They lied about where we needed to go, knowing the weather would make it impossible to get to the correct location in time. We were a few days late but he took the oath anyway. On his knees. They have wanted to kill our clan for a long time. The government demands loyalty to the king, not to clan chiefs. They fear the power of the united clan. Staying together is our greatest strength."

Many of our clanspeople answered John's small speech with prideful boasts and short-lived chanting. My mind tried to understand what he had said. The king ordered my grandfather killed? I hoped John would not change his mind about returning to the glen. The king could get away with secret orders for a time but when the story got out that he ordered his own citizens murdered, public opinion would force him to blame someone else and return our lands to us. Right? John had to bring us back home so we could claim our rightful property.

John and my Father sat by the fire discussing our options. The rest of us returned to our chores.

Mother and I went to our shelter before Father and John were finished with their discussion. Mother looked tired and I could not remember the last time I saw her eat anything. When we got home, I would make sure to do all the chores that required standing and ask Father to build a wee stool for Mother to rest on while she worked.

At some point in the dark night, our third and final night in the camp in the woods, I went to the fire to warm my rock. Mother did not stir when I got up. Perhaps her rock was not cold enough to wake her yet.

"Dory, good," Father said when he saw me. "I was hoping to talk to you before I left."

My stomach jumped. "You're leaving for the glen in the middle of the night?" I asked. "Why not wait for the sun?"

"I am not going to the glen. I am headed to Edinburgh. John thinks we need a presence there to get our side of the story out and force the king's hand. I will negotiate on behalf of the clan."

"Why cannae John go? He is the chief."

"He needs to be with the clan, to make the decisions here."

"We better practice your French, then. And Latin for if you meet with the church."

"There is no time, lass. The quicker I set out, the faster we will know if we are safe in the glen. I will get by."

The idea of not being safe in the glen was too difficult to understand. Even though I had watched my clansmen murdered in our baile, it was home. The safest place I knew.

Father had been a chief's son and was now the chief's brother, which meant his time was devoted to the whole clan. It made me proud, even though I knew the dangers involved in his missions. Every time Father left us, even if it was on a simple cattle raid, we knew it could be the last time we saw each other. This time when he hugged me there was a special sadness. He wanted to return to the glen as much as I did, I thought. Still, he seemed extra concerned about leaving.

I added an extra squeeze to my hug, to make him feel better. Then I went back to sleep.

My chattering teeth woke me as weak sunbeams filtered into the otherwise empty shelter. Morning. The morning of our return to the glen. I felt uneasy and confused but did not know why. Sleep muddled my mind.

When I got to the fire, the mood in camp was subdued. Perhaps it was the thought of extinguishing the fire that made people anxious. I was not looking forward to the freezing walk back either, but we were headed home to rebuild.

"Where is everyone?" I asked John. He was busy packing a few small sacks and tying them to a long leather strap.

"The Hendersons are headed to Appin. We will need more supplies and help from their scouts. I also arranged for a funereal boat for MacIain. I doubt Glenlyon's men left enough in the baile to make a boat and MacIain will be buried on Eilean Munde where he belongs."

Eilean Munde was the traditional burial ground for the chiefs of a few clans, not just ours. The island was in the middle of Loch Leven, the large loch west of Glencoe. MacIain would rest, undisturbed in a cairn, a burial made of rocks.

"I am ready, sir," Calum said. He had appeared at the chief's side.

"Good, lad," John said. "I'm counting on you to get this done for me. Greenock is far and there will be Redcoats looking for Glencoe MacDonalds to punish."

"Aye, I won't let you down, sir." Calum had never stood so straight in his whole life. What was going on?

"Sir, you sent Father to Edinburgh and the Henderson to Appin. Now you send Calum to Greenock? You said we had to stay together, that the clan had to stay united."

"And I meant that, Dory. But things have changed."

"Overnight, sir?" I asked. "Where is Mother?"

"Gone, lass."

"Gone? Where did you send her? Why did you not send me with her?"

"I did not send her. The Lord sent for her."

My stomach turned to stone and dropped.

"Dead?" My voice wavered as I spoke. "Mother is dead?"

"Same as the others. She was too sick to make it in this cold."

"It is *not* the same!" I yelled. "She is *my mother*!"

"I am sorry, Dory." His tone made me lower my head. "I am. Your mother was a good woman. Nevertheless, there are matters of the clan to attend. I cannae find out how serious the danger is if I have to worry about you. Your father and I discussed it before he left. If your mother did not make it through the night, you had to go to the New World."

I dropped to my knees.

"Leave Scotland?" I asked. Surely, I had heard him wrong.

"Go with Calum," John said. "Go to Greenock. It will be a long, hard journey and you must stay hidden as much as possible. Once there, get on a ship to Massachusetts territory. You can live with your Aunt Orlie and her husband."

"How can you send me away, sir? What about Father? He will need me when he gets back from Edinburgh. My place is here. In Scotland, in the glen."

"Do not question me, Dory," he warned. "Go." He draped the leather strap with hanging bags around my neck like a sash. "Be safe."

We were both silent for a few moments, except that I sniffled like a baby. How could this be happening? Was Mother dead? Could I be sent away from my home forever? Would I ever see my family ever again?

"When may I come back, sir?" I asked.

"Probably never," he said the truth in his direct way. He looked pained by what he was doing to me but that did not make me feel any better about it. "Remember you are a MacIain, a MacDonald of Glencoe. Make us proud."

Chapter Six

If my heart had not already been broken and scattered in the wind, I would have bawled like a newborn. My head was spinning. Mother *dead*? Father sending me away, far, far away, across an ocean to people I have never met and who have never met me? How could this be happening? I wanted to go back home with everyone else and help win our land and honor back from the English. I wanted to stay, rebuild and fight, not run and hide like a baby. But I was a member of the clan and the chief had given me an order. My father, the second in command, had okayed it.

It seemed I had no choice. As Calum and I walked with our backs to the path back home, I somehow knew that the glen had not finished seeing tragedies.

Calum as my guide and escort. That was a laugh. He was the most timid lad in the glen or who had ever visited the glen. He was shorter than me by at least an inch and had chicken legs. If we ran into trouble, it would be up to me to think fast and get us out of it.

We were a few minutes out of camp, when I went numb. Not my feet, more like my whole body, especially where my heart used to be.

"Sorry about your mother," he said. I said nothing. What could I say?

A few minutes later, we passed a low heap of rocks. A cairn. A grave. I wondered if it was my mother or Gilbert's mother. Then another disturbing thought. Was it both of them? I let the tears fall down my cheeks and gather at my chin. I wiped my nose with the rags wrapped around my hands.

This was absurd. How could I let them send me away? There had to be a way to convince my father and my uncle that I should not go to the New World. The glen needed me as much as I needed it. Even more now with both Mother and Gilbert dead. I had to get Calum to turn around and go back to the glen. If I was sly about, I might be able to trick him. Of course, trickery may not be needed. He was weak-willed and might give in if I badgered him enough.

I glanced over at him, trying to judge which path I should attempt. Calum was annoying even when he was quiet. He kept looking at the trees over his shoulder. With his head turned, he would walk right in front of me or into me. Then he would apologize, blush and walk normal for a few steps before staring over his shoulder again. Could he not walk straight like a normal person? About the tenth time he walked into me I stopped.

"What is it?" I snapped. "What are you looking for?"

"Sorry," he said. We started walking again.

"I did not ask for an apology, I asked what you are looking for."

"I do not want to tell you. You will think I have gone mad."

"Too late. You might as well tell me."

Calum took a deep breath. "Something is following me."

"Who?" I looked around for the flash of a red coat.

"Not who. What."

"You mean like an elf?"

"No."

"What then, a wraith or a fairy?"

"No," he replied. "I would not be able to see a wraith."

"That would not mean it was not there. When a leaf moves from one place to another how did it get there?"

"The wind," Calum offered.

"But you cannae see the wind. How do you know it was not a mischievous invisible wraith?"

"Dory!" Calum was easy to frustrate. It may be harder to get him to turn around than I thought.

"All I mean is it was not a ridiculous suggestion that you were being followed by something you could not see."

"I can see it."

"Oh. Come on, then. What is it?"

Calum took a deep breath, lowering his eyes toward his boots.

"A bird."

"A bird," I repeated. "You are afraid of a tiny little bird?"

"This is no ordinary bird." Calum raised his head to look me straight in the eyes. "It is cunning. Every time I turn 'round, there it is."

Awwk! Awwk!

We both turned at the sound and sure enough, there was a bird. Calum was right about another thing, too. It was not just any bird.

It was Merlin!

"Merlin!"

He landed on the ground behind us, his back straight, neck stiff and beautiful feathers tucked close. I could tell by his posture that he was indignant at having been left behind but in exchange for a good meal would forgive me at once. Had I had a small bird or vole, I would have given it to him with pleasure.

"Merlin?" Calum asked. "Your bird has been following me since I left the glen."

The moment I was sure it was Merlin, my Merlin, a mighty gust of wind blew up from nowhere and almost knocked me over. Instead, it brought the pieces of my heart fluttering back to me. They reformed in my chest and for a moment, I felt pure joy. Then, in a blink, all the pain, sorrow, loss and madness of the last few days hit me like the heaviest boulder. Perhaps my heart had not reformed in full. It felt like there were empty spaces in it.

My knees buckled and I fell to the ground sobbing.

"Dory," Calum said, panic slipping into his voice. He put his hand on my back. "We have to keep going. There's no cover here and only a few hours of sun before we need to make camp."

I knew he was right but could not move, could not breathe. The pain was crushing. Most of my family had been murdered, including my beloved mother, my grandest grandfather, and my best friend. Our home had burned. Now I must leave Scotland and would never see my glen again. My father's fate may never be known to me. All I had was Merlin.

Oh, how my heart ached! I longed to be numb again. Feeling the pain hurt much worse.

And yet, I was so happy to have Merlin back. How could he have survived the fire? How did he escape his cage?

"Come on," Calum said. He was looking over his shoulder, this time for Redcoats. "Keep moving."

Between his coaxing and tugging, he got me to my feet and moving again. We trudged along, me leaning on Calum because my knees were still too shaky to hold me. How did Merlin get out? I kept asking myself.

"I think I know how your bird escaped," Calum said. It appeared I had been muttering aloud.

"You do?" I asked, turning to face him. I tightened my grip on his arm. "Tell me."

"The morning of the attack was so confusing," he said. "People were screaming, crying out in pain, yelling out orders. Animals were trying to escape, too, running in all directions. Gilbert chased the animals out of his burning house. Then he ran screaming into your bothie. A Redcoat followed him in. I ran to help Gilbert but before I got there, Merlin flew out the door. I heard a horrible sound that twisted my stomach and then the Redcoat came out, blood dripping from his bayonet. He grabbed a lit torch and set your roof on fire.

"He turned and saw me." Calum's voice was softer now. "He said something to me but I could not quite hear it. Then he aimed his gun at me, the knife on the end wet with the blood of my friend. I was a coward. I ran. I ran straight up the hill, up a path we had all run together hundreds of times. I knew which way to go and the soldier followed as best he could but kept losing his footing. He even fired a shot at me but missed when he slipped on a patch of ice. I ran and ran and ran. Finally, I hid by the burn where the Hendersons found me."

It was too much. My thoughts whirling inside my head, I vomited. There was little in my stomach so I dry-heaved and a terrible taste filled my mouth.

Gilbert had saved Merlin. He knew how I treasured my bird and Gilbert died saving him. He could have run like Calum and the rest of us but he chose to stay and save as many animals as he could.

I loved Merlin but wished my friend had saved himself.

Chapter Seven

Calum and I walked until we reached the edge of the next forest. It snowed on and off but the wind blew all day. I shivered and my throat was scratchy from crying. Merlin was nowhere to be seen.

"I'll make the fire, you get the oats ready," Calum said.

He looked around the ground for firewood.

"What oats?" I asked. "Where would I have gotten food?"

"The sacks the chief gave you." He pointed to the leather strap around my shoulder. "One of them has oats in it. Did he not tell you?"

"No." Irritated at Calum's confidence, I jiggled the first sack and heard jingling. Coins. The second one was soft and made no noise. Inside was a big pile of oats. There was a small stone at the bottom. I knew that stone. This was not just an oat sack it was my family's oat sack. Mother had put the stone in it to keep the oats fresh. My heart ached a bit more when I thought of my mother. John had not given us some of the clan's food supply, he had given us my family's food. I may be the last one left to eat it.

Calum looked in his own backsack and handed over a small jug of water plugged with a cork.

"You didn't want to tell me about this when I was thirsty enough to melt snow in my mouth?"

"We need the good water to make oatcakes," Calum said. "That's more important."

I wanted to argue but he was right. Snow was good enough to wet our throats as we walked.

I looked around for Merlin. My thick leather glove, strong leather ties and his cage were back in the glen. That meant I had no control over Merlin. Not that I ever did. Merlin had always fought against his restraints. When I put him in his cage, he would mope and turn his body so his back was toward me no matter where I stood. But when he was out in the fields, hunting, watching, moving on the wind, he always came when I called. Not immediately, but soon enough.

"Birds need to be free," Gilbert had taught me. "They hate being confined, told when to eat, when to sleep, when to work. Don't be afraid to give him his freedom."

I searched the evergreens for a glimpse of his beak. His darker feathers blended with the bark and the snow would hide his white tail feathers. His yellow beak would stand out against the trees. Nothing. I hoped Gilbert was right about giving Merlin his freedom.

Calum was doing his best to start a fire for us. He found a fallen evergreen branch and used it like a broom to clear an area of snow. He broke the branch into smaller pieces and set them in the middle of the clearing. Then he took out his flint and started striking it against his steel dagger. I set about my own jobs, finding a high tree hollow to hide the bags and shaking out the blankets. Moving around was better than standing motionless, staring at Calum. Time after time, strike after strike, tiny little sparks jumped off his blade but died in the air. The wind howled its victories. Calum muttered to himself but kept trying as his fingers turned red and then white from the cold.

I was about to step in when the kindling started to smoke and then glowed. Calum protected it with his hands from the howling wind and blew on it, adding twigs. Soon, a small flame burned. Once the fire was large enough to give off heat, Merlin appeared on a nearby rock. Bits of blood and skin from whatever small creature had been his meal dotted his beak and crown feathers.

"Merlin!" I scolded. "Where have you been?" We both knew I was more relieved to see him then angry. He stood calmly, bending his right leg, resting his whole body weight on his left.

"Crazy bird," I muttered.

When feeling returned to our fingers, Calum pulled a small pan out of his sack. I poured a bit of water into small piles of oats, put them in the pan and placed the pan near the fire. Calum walked a short distance away from the fire searching the ground.

"What are you looking for now?" I asked.

"Rocks," he said. "Sleeping rocks."

As Calum searched, I watched the oatcakes. I remembered all the times I had stood next to my mother as we made the family meals together. Father always told me how much I looked like her, tall, as most Highlanders were, with long dark brown hair and grey eyes. The biggest difference, he would say, was that my hair showed the red color of our ancestors when the light hit it. With a stick, I poked at the oatcakes to prevent them from burning as even more tears trickled down my cheeks.

Later as Calum and I ate our meager meal, memories of Gilbert bringing small jugs of sweet honey to our door jumped up in my mind. My stomach turned and I feared it would empty again. I swallowed hard and tried to calm my nerves.

"Need some water?" Calum asked.

"No." I was still angry with Calum for no good reason. Besides, I had not figured out how to get him to turn back.

We were silent for a while longer, listening to the sounds of the woods. There were animals all over, some drawn by the fire, others frightened by it. I heard a distant howl.

"Was that a wolf?" Calum asked. Apparently, nighttime brought out his timid side.

"Not likely," I said. "The wolf hunts have nearly wiped them out. It is the wind."

We heard the noise again. There were other sounds. Owls hooting, leaves rustling, branches moaning from the strain of fighting the wind. A vole ran out from nearby bushes and scurried passed the fire. The bushes continued to rustle. Something larger than a mouse was in there.

"Dory," Calum whispered.

"I see it." He had left his dagger on a nearby rock. I took it in my right hand and motioned to him with my left. He picked up the branch I pointed to and lit it, holding it like a torch. I tried to remember all the fireside stories of warriors like Queen Maeve that I had heard through the years. She was brave and bold and feared nothing. How I wished I were her.

"Is it a wildcat?" Calum asked.

"It's too big," I said.

"A deer than? An enormous buck? What do you think it is?"

"People. They either want our food, which we do not have, our fire, or..."

"Or what?"

"Or they are Redcoats who wants us dead."

Chapter Eight

Calum and I stood with torch and dagger in hand, ready to fight for our lives. I wanted Calum to call out something, maybe that we were a huge band of roving bandits, ready and eager to take whatever they were carrying. The Timid One stood frozen instead. This time I resisted the urge to check his legs for urine stains.

I deepened my voice as best I could and called, "State your business!"

The rustling continued. It did not seem like the people in the brush were anxious to come out. I hoped to scare them away.

"I have my pistol aimed at you! State your business or prepare to die!"

More seconds passed. The rustling stopped. Had they left? Had I scared them off?

Suddenly, two figures leapt from the brush. Calum jumped back, screaming. Lucky for the attackers, he did not drop the torch. If he had extinguished the light, I would have run the knife through Roderick Henderson before I saw his smarmy face. He and Ian were rolling on the ground laughing.

"I almost killed you!" I yelled. My body was wet with sweat from fear. Now that the danger was over, I could feel the cold again. I shivered and coughed.

"With your p-pistol?" Ian managed to say through his laughter.

I kicked him in the side on my way back to the fire to get warm.

Calum stood frozen. The look on his face was pure disbelief.

"You scared us, on purpose?" he asked. "Why? How is that funny?"

"You're just sore because you were the one getting scared this time," Ian said.

"Come to think of it, he's the one who gets scared all the time isn't he?" Roderick asked. This brought another bout of laughing.

Calum joined me to warm by the fire.

"Give me my dagger," he whispered. "I will kill them now, I swear it."

"Not a chance," I said. I tucked it in my skirt's waistband where I planned to keep it.

"What are you doing here, anyway?" I asked. "Are you not supposed to be in Appin getting supplies? Why are you roaming the woods? Are you lost?"

"Hah!" Roderick said. "Hendersons are known for not getting lost."

"Actually, Hendersons are known for spinning tales," I corrected him. I could not stop the smile that spread across my face. Their father was our seannachie, the one who told the clan's stories at evening fires.

"Not funny," Ian said. "Maybe we'll say we couldn't find you after all."

"You are looking for us?" I asked. "Did John change his mind? Did he say to bring us back?" I pictured myself back in the glen helping to rebuild our home. Roderick dashed the hope as soon as it sprung up in my heart.

"We were in Appin, remember?" Roderick said. "There will be a boat filled with supplies from Stewarts on the way up Loch Leven tomorrow. We are going to a few more places in the morning before we head for the glen. The chief would want us to report to him if we saw you."

A marvelous thought came to me. I could use this situation to get back to Glencoe. There is no way Calum would stand up to all three of us. If I could get the Henderson lads to say I should come back, Calum would back down for sure.

"You thought it would be fun to sneak up on us?" Calum asked.

"We were sneaking because we were not sure it was you," Ian said. "When Dory started threatening us in her man voice, we could not resist the chance to scare you. It was in good fun."

Ian and Roderick picked through the brush to find everything they had dropped, two sacks, two plaids and one plain blanket.

"No need to offer us any food," Roderick said. "We ate with a Stewart family. Meat dripping with juices, potatoes the size of my fist. Fresh milk. Mmmmm. Delicious."

He was exaggerating I was sure. He wanted to make us more miserable than we were. It worked. I could not stop thinking about a big delicious meal or how I would never share one with my family ever again.

"I wonder how things are back in the glen," I ventured.

"Cold and miserable," Roderick said. "Same as here."

"What do you have in the sacks?" Ian asked.

"Supplies," Calum said. His defensive tone was not subtle.

"We are not going to rob you," Ian said. "I was just curious."

"Coins in one, oats in the other," I said to end the conversation, trying to return it to Glencoe.

"There are three, Dory," Ian reminded me.

"Oh, right." I lifted the third sack. Whatever was inside was very light. I opened it and could not believe what I saw. I reached in and pulled out a smoky yellowish-brown gemstone hanging from a long, thin leather tie.

"What is it?" Calum asked.

"My mother's necklace," I said. It reflected the small fire and seemed to burn from within. Mother loved that necklace and I often begged her to let me wear it. She told me one day it would be mine. We had both expected that day to be many years from now. I dropped the sack and tied the necklace around my neck, knotting it thrice to keep it in place. The weight of the stone on my chest was strange.

"What kind of stone is that?" Roderick asked.

"A cairngorm," I said. "From the mountains way north and east of Glencoe. My grandfather, my mother's father, got some in a trade and gave one to each of his children."

"I guess the chief wanted you to have a part of Scotland to take with you," Calum said.

"That is not why he gave it to me," I said. I knew what it was for as soon as I saw it. "It is rare for someone from our part of the Highlands to have a cairngorm."

"True," Ian said. "I do not know anyone who's even seen one other than yours."

"How does that explain why the chief gave it to you?" Roderick asked.

"It is the only way to prove who I am to my aunt in the New World."

We were all silent for a while. The animal noises continued as I thought about the weight of what I had said.

I had to leave Scotland and cross the ocean to a strange land where I knew no one. In the glen, everyone knew me as the granddaughter and now niece of the chief. In America, I would need to prove who I was. After I figured it out.

The lads were quiet, looking from one to another. I was not going to be able to convince them to let me go back to the glen, now. I needed rest.

"Since you scared us," I said, breaking the silence, "you can take the first watch."

Calum and I grabbed our sleeping rocks from next to the fire. With Calum's dagger in my hand, I went a few feet deeper into the forest where there were more trees. I found a tree trunk without too much snow around it. I wrapped myself in my plaid, held my rock to my stomach, sat down with my back against the tree and tried to sleep.

None of us slept well. We were all up and down throughout the night, trying to keep warm. I spend most of the night rubbing the cairngorm now dangling from my neck. My mind raced with thoughts of my mother, Gilbert, my grandfather and even my father. Too soon, there was enough morning light fighting through the grey clouds to start moving again.

This was my last chance to get the Hendersons on my side about returning to the glen.

I rolled over and felt a zing of pain as something hard jabbed into my backside. I reached under my blanket and pulled out a small rock. I was about to toss it aside when I noticed it was smoothed to a pointy tip. This was no rock. It was an elf-bolt. In spite of my current situation, I smiled. Finding one of these elfin weapons meant elves had been fighting nearby. When Gilbert and I found one, we would hide behind the heather and wait for a battle to come our way. Which side were they fighting for today? I dropped the bolt in the now empty sack that had held my mother's necklace. Back to the task at hand, I shook snow, mouse droppings and pine needles off my plaid and wrapped it around my shoulders.

We ate a slow oatmeal breakfast.

"Guess this will be it then?" Ian said as we ate.

"I suppose. Unless you get all the way back to the glen and John, I mean the chief, sends you back out after us."

"Why would he do that?" Roderick asked.

"In case he changes his mind about sending me to the New World. He could decide that I should be back in the glen, helping to get it rebuilt."

"It is weird when you think about it," Ian said. "We all thought we would live our whole lives in the glen. Now, who knows? Maybe none of us will. Maybe the king will send his men again someday."

No, no, no. This was not the way the conversation should go.

"My father is on his way to negotiate for us right now. He will need my help when he returns."

The lads ignored me. Ian continued his thought.

"And you two have a long journey to even get to Greenock. If you make it, who knows if Calum here can make it back without you."

The Hendersons were teasing Calum, of course, but was a grain of truth in what they said.

"I had not thought of that. See, Calum, we should go back and make sure this is what they want."

"Oh, it is." Roderick said. "I was warming my rock when I heard them talking. Your father wants you out of Scotland and safe with your aunt and uncle. He said it is what your mother would want. You are a direct heir to the MacIain."

His words twisted my stomach. What my mother would want? For me to be separated from Father? Can that be? What did my being a direct heir to my grandfather have to do with anything?

I needed time to think these new ideas over in my mind.

Once the fire was out, the lads and I exchanged solemn nods. Parting ways without another word, Ian and Roderick headed north, Calum and I headed south.

Chapter Nine

Our journey was excruciating and slow. We walked during the day, resting at night. Trekking through snow and ice day after day was exhausting. We traveled short distances each day. At times, the snow came down so hard the whole world looked white. This had to be the worst winter Scotland had ever seen.

In the glen, when it snowed, we just stayed inside for a day, two at the most. Out here on the journey, there was no inside, nowhere to hide from the wind and the snow. No clan gatherings, either. It was lonely, just Calum, Merlin and me.

Once in a while deep snowdrifts trapped us in one of our makeshift camps. One time we waited half a week for the snow to melt a bit. Within an hour of setting out again, it started snowing, a hard snow with blowing winds that made it difficult to see where we were going. Were we even on the right path? We had not seen another person in many days. I had barely seen Merlin. Once a day he showed himself, resting on a tree branch or frozen rock. It was a relief whenever he showed.

"How do you think everyone is doing back home?" I asked.

"They are cold, hungry and tired like we are," Calum answered. He squinted through the blowing snow, studying our surroundings with furrowed brow.

"At least they have loads of people around," I said.

"Loads of people to bury, too."

Mother was not buried in her proper place. She was not even in the glen. Would they go back and get her or would she stay in an unmarked grave by the side of the road?

"I wish we were back there helping," I said.

"Mmmm," was his response. Calum was not catching on to my hints.

"They could use our help," I added. "Especially yours, being one of the few lads left."

He continued to squint as we walked.

"I think we should go back," I told him flat out.

Calum stopped. I stopped, too. For a moment, I thought he was going to yell at me, insisting we could never go back.

"You are right," he said.

What? My heart beat faster. Could it be that easy? All I had to do was say we should go back and the Timid One agreed?

"Great!" I said and turned around before he could change his mind. To my great surprised, he followed me.

"I do not see why this is great," he muttered.

"Not to worry," I said. "It will work out."

"Why are you happy? I thought you would be angry we got lost."

"I am happy to be going home!"

"That is a surprise. I did not think you would ever call the New World home."

"What are you talking about?" Then something Calum had said moments earlier hit me. "Lost? Did you say we were lost?"

"Aye, yeah," he said. "That is why we have to go back."

"To the glen," I said.

"No. Back to the turn we missed. I think it was covered with snow."

"I thought we were going back home, to the glen," I said. Fear, anger, disappointment bubbled up from my chest and threatened to spew out my mouth. I could not stop the tears. "Why cannae we go home?"

"We are," Calum said. "We are going to your new home. The chief gave me an order and I will follow it. Although, I am not following it very well right now since I got us lost." He had taken the lead again and was walking faster. The snow continued to swirl around us even as the wind slowed.

"You know home is the glen!" I yelled. I was out of control. Before I knew it, my fists were beating on Calum's chest. "Please, let us go home. I need to go back. I cannae live without the clan. Please, Calum, please."

He did not say anything. He caught my hands and held them in the air. Anger and frustration melted into exhaustion. I was not going home. I would not ever see the glen again. I fell into him, crying like a child on his shoulder. He let me cry for a while. Then just started walking again. I spent the rest of the day in a trance, following Calum without a word.

That night I had a terrible half-dream, half-memory. Dark figures dancing around a roaring blaze. The memory was from a few nights before the horrible attack. The amount of mead and claret Glenlyon's men had drunk made them senseless of the snow on the ground and the icy wind. They were in various states of dress as kilts, shirts and cloaks had been shrugged off in the dance.

In my dream, the fire distorted their shadows into grotesque creatures prancing on the snow. They looked like the devil's minions dancing between the fire and the ice. One by one, the creatures left the fire and crept toward me. I tried to run but my feet were stuck to the ground in pools of blood. My heart beat faster, I yelled for help. Gilbert! Mother! MacIain! No one came. They were all dead. I was alone and the creatures leapt at me.

I woke to the sound of my own screaming.

Calum woke, too, or was already awake.

"Are you okay?" he asked in a controlled voice that made my blood boil with rage. Why was I such a mess and he was calm?

"It was a bad dream, I think."

"What else would it be?"

"You know, a message, a premonition. Something like that."

"You mean something magic?" Calum asked.

"Supernatural at least."

"You know I do not deal in the supernatural if I can help it."

"Believing in the supernatural, is believing in things you cannae see."

"That is called faith and faith is religion, not magic. Dealing in the supernatural is asking for trouble."

"Incantations, spells, trying to manipulate nature for your own gain, that's bad, wicked even. Doing those things to help people is good. Like healers. You believe in healers do you not?"

"They use plants and animals in certain ways to heal sickness, not invisible creatures."

"Believing in help from creatures you cannae see is normal, nothing supernatural or bad about it. " I said. "I do not know how you get on in this world with that attitude, Calum."

"You would be surprised."

"We better get moving."

It took us three days to climb up and down Beinn Fhionnlaidh. It was a big mountain with dangerous slopes and gullies where snow and ice piled high. We had been headed south for weeks before we even reached the base of Beinn Fhionnlaidh. I think we walked in circles because Calum insisted he take the lead.

It snowed a bit each day but the wind was not as harsh, which was good since there were not as many trees to block it. However, this caused another problem. We were hiding from anyone who might be looking for escaped Glencoe MacDonalds. Redcoats, for sure, but there were others who did not favor our clan. Being cattle rustlers and supporters of the ousted king did not make us popular outside our own glen. Of course, we had no idea from what direction Redcoats or angry Highlanders might be coming. It was difficult to hide behind whatever large rocks and small hills we could find, when we did not know where the front was.

In the middle of the afternoon on the second day, Calum was

walking a few paces in front me in a narrow passage.

"Ahh!"

I glanced up and Calum was gone.

"Dory!" he cried. I crept forward a few steps and looked down toward Calum's voice. His shoulders were even with the snow line. He had fallen through a snow pile up to his neck. "I cannae feel my feet!"

"Okay," I said. "Stay calm. We will get you out."

I dug a little around his shoulders so he could move them. Calum struggled to get his right arm free. I had to be careful how much snow I removed. We had no idea how deep the hole went. If I removed too much snow, he could slide out of reach and be gone forever.

"Careful, careful." I told him as he crept the other arm free. Between him squirming a bit and me pulling on his arms and then his torso, he climbed out of the hole in a few minutes. By the time he was safe, he was also soaked to the skin and in need of a fire.

Chapter Ten

As I watched Calum's lips turn from blue to white, which was an improvement, what Roderick had said all those nights ago weighed on my mind. If this was what my mother and my father both wanted for me, then I should honor their request.

But what if I knew in my heart that they were wrong to send me away? Living in the glen was not easy but everyone had a task and we did it. I could not read any documents or write any letters, but the MacIain taught me to speak and understand languages better than anyone left in the glen did. We speak Gaelic among ourselves and other Highlanders, Scots with Lowlanders, French and English are needed for dealing with the Crown and European leaders and Latin is used for some negotiating in religious circles. Who would help them now? And what would I do in the New World? Who would I be? I doubted my being a blood heir to the MacIain would help me across the ocean.

If Calum and I got to Greenock, and at this point that was a big question, then I had to convince him to let us go to Edinburgh before I got on a ship. With my knowledge of languages and government policies, I could find my father and plead my case. Maybe I could get him to change his mind if I talked to him in person.

I tried to pick up our pace a bit. Now that I had a new plan, I wanted to get to Greenock with enough time to convince Calum to go to Edinburgh, too.

"Of all times to be wearing trews," Calum muttered.

I knew what he meant. The further south we walked, the more trees, bushes, heather and brush we had to walk through. Winter had stripped the branches back to bare thorny twigs and bramble. My skirts snagged with every step. The same was happening to Calum's pants. If he had been wearing his kilt when he fled the killing, the bottom of the plaid would float above most of the thorny branches allowing him to move quicker and his thick socks would protect his lower legs from the scratches. For the first time, I wished I could wear a kilt.

Calum had started staring at me when he thought I was not looking. I remembered when Gilbert used to steal looks at me. One day last autumn, we were in the heather, studying bees. The sun was shining brighter than ever. Gilbert had smiled at me awkwardly just as a breeze brushed over my skin. I thought he might kiss me. Instead, Roderick Henderson came racing through the field waving a fish he had speared with a sharpened stick. I had liked it when Gilbert looked at me. Calum's look was different. Strange. I did not like it.

"Dory," Calum asked. "Do you feel alright?"

"Fine," I answered without thinking. "Why?"

"Your face is red. And you are slurring your words a bit. Are you tired?"

"No." I snapped. Of course, I was tired. I had not had a true night's sleep in weeks and would not get one for many more. How could he say I was slurring? I sounded fine to me. "Maybe you're the one who's not doing well. If you want to stop, just say so."

Calum said nothing. He kept walking. Soon we could see the swirling smoke from a chimney off to our left.

"Maybe we should stop and rest," he said.

"We have a little more time before the sun sets," I told him. I was annoyed because my feet kept slipping on the icy ground.

"Maybe we should check out that house," Calum said. "They may let us stay the night for a few coins."

"We need to save our coins," I told him. "Nous n'avons pas de temps. We have to keep going."

"What did you say?"

"There's not much time. We have to keep going."

"You were speaking in a different language for a sentence. I think it was French. You are acting feverish. Maybe we should save our coins for a healer in the next village."

The scratchy throat had become a burning, my head pounded, my body was sweaty in spite of the cold weather and I felt dizzy. I *was* sick. I hated being sick and I hated Calum being right again even more.

"Fine," I said. "We can ask at the small house for some real food and a good night's sleep inside. Happy?"

"Hardly, but I will take it. When we get there, let me do the talking."

"No way. You will wind up giving away all of our money."

"I do not even know how much we have."

"There is a reason for that. I will do the talking."

"How will we know if it is safe to talk to them?" Calum asked.

"We will not tell them who we are or where we are from. In fact, we should hide the plaid under the plain blanket."

"What if they ask?"

I rolled my eyes but he was right. Best to be prepared.

"Our names will be…" I glanced around trying to think of a name. "Forest. We are Dory and Cal Forest, brother and sister on our way to Glasgow."

"Fine," he muttered. "If they shoot at us, head southeast toward the next village. We will meet up there."

"Fine." I did not point out that if they shot at us they would hit and kill us. I took a coin out of my sack and palmed it. I turned the leather sash so the sacks hung at my back hidden from sight under the blanket I held wrapped around my body.

The closer we got to the house tucked into a hillside the more detail I could see. Icicles hung on the eaves looking like perfect sugar sticks. Through the window, I could see the glow of a nice fire. There appeared to be one person moving around inside. The front door had a red and white striped circle hanging on it. Just before we knocked, I could swear I smelled shortbread.

Knock! Knock!

A few moments passed before the door squeaked open. Wonderful smells wafted out at us. Pastries, coffee and the familiar odor of burning peat reminded me of home. I wanted to cry. Again.

"Pardon me, ma'am," I said. She had one eye with the other socket sewn shut with black thread. Her back curved toward the ground and I began to think it was her body and not the door that had creaked. "We are sorry to bother you. We have been traveling for many days and wondered if you had any food to spare."

"Oh, my," she said in a shaky voice. "I will find something to feed you children. Come in, come in, you poor souls. It is too mean to be out in this weather."

"Thank you ma'am," I said. After stepping inside, I almost fell to the floor. It was wonderful to be sheltered again. The wind was not whipping at my face and the sounds of the animals were distant and less threatening once the door closed.

"Come, sit," the old woman cooed. "I will find some fine food for you." She took a red blanket and hung it across the window. "It helps keep the chill out."

"We can offer one coin," I told her. "I fear it is all we have."

"My dear, I have no need for coins. You can however, pay your way by doing a few chores for me. Once you are rested and fed, of course."

"What kind of chores?" Calum asked.

"Chopping and fetching firewood, clearing ashes out from the fireplace and perhaps you could chase away the cobwebs from the corners, lass. My eyes are not as sharp as they once were and I cannot stand an untidy home."

I glanced around the small house. Not a thing was out of place and I did not see any cobwebs. Calum looked at me with a small smile. Doing simple chores in exchange for meat and warmth? That was a great deal.

"Aye, ma'am. It will be our pleasure to help."

"Aye ma'am." Calum added. "What would you like us to do first?"

The old woman went to the fire and pulled out a fresh batch of shortbread.

"Eat. You have come just in time. I was doing a little baking. My son will be coming to visit me sometime soon and I like to have sweets for him."

"Oh, ma'am. We would not want to eat the sweets meant for your son."

"Tish, tish. There is plenty here. I am not eating the way I used to. Getting older, you know. Eat up. Eat up."

I had been hoping for a nice stew with meat and vegetables but the shortbread was delicious. The most delicious shortbread I had ever eaten. It must have tasted so good because all we had had for weeks was oats and water. My fingers were warming up and my head stopped pounding quite so hard. I expected to feel energized as I ate but instead, I became sleepy. Calum's eyes were closing as we sat at the table.

"You are welcome to lie down and rest your heads," the old woman told us, "after you finish up here." She pulled a tin down from a shelf and pulled biscuits out. "These are my son's favorites. He can spare a few. Last I saw him, he was getting a little thick around the middle. You two need all the sweets you can get. Eat up. Eat up."

My stomach was full but my mind wanted to eat. Eat as much as I could while I was warm and safe. The thought of lying down with a real straw bed under me almost too much to bear. With each bite, I got sleepier and sleepier.

"Just keep eating, my dears," the old woman said. "Then you can rest. After that we will get you in the fireplace."

Calum's eyelids snapped open. "*In* the fireplace, ma'am?" he asked.

"To clean it, of course," she said with a weak smile. "Warm milk with a bit of cocoa?"

I notice she had not sat since we arrived. She busied herself around the house finding more sweets to feed us. Something started to feel strange. Most adults would have feed us meat and charged coins up front. Was she just a kind old woman? Calum fought to keep his eyes open and following the woman around the small space. He thought something was off, too.

"Ma'am? Maybe we could do some of those chores for you now." I said.

"No, you are not ready, yet. Just keep eating."

"Maybe we could lie down for a moment," I said. "It is so cozy in here and I am very weary."

"I believe sister has a fever, ma'am," Calum said, noticing my cue. "It might be best if she rests."

"Oh, dear but you do look a little pale. Go on and rest. The bed is large enough for three grown people. My son takes good care of me, that is for certain."

Calum and I went behind the hanging tattered blanket used to divide the small home. We sat on the edge of the straw bed. It felt glorious beneath me and I longed to stretch out on it.

"We have to get out of here," Calum whispered. "I think she means to cook us."

Chapter Eleven

I could not believe this old woman would do anything as gruesome as that but I did agree she seemed a bit strange.

"Alright, we can go," I said. Calum stood up, looking toward the side door. The old woman started singing to herself. It was a soft tune. Nothing I recognized but somehow comforting and familiar.

"Wait. What if we are wrong?" I said.

"What?"

"What if she is a nice old woman who wanted to give us sweets? It would be dishonorable to run out on her without paying our end of the debt."

Calum paused for a moment. Then nodded. Glencoe MacDonalds believed in honor. "Fine. What do you want to do?"

"The firewood," I said. "At least then you will have a weapon. You chop and I will stack it. We stay where we can see each other."

"You should rest, though," Calum said. "You do not look good."

The bed felt soft and comfortable beneath me. I wanted to curl up under my blanket and sleep for weeks. However, rest would do me no good if the old woman were out to harm us.

"I can rest outside where you can see me while you chop."

We ducked out the side door and walked over to the chopping stump. As Calum was setting up, I heard noises coming from the front of the house. Footsteps and voices.

"Quiet, Calum," I whispered. "Someone's coming."

Calum held onto the axe and followed me as I crept along the side of the house. The sweets in my stomach turned sour. I reached up to touch my mother's necklace. Feeling it gave me comfort. I peeked around the corner and saw Redcoats.

I mouthed "red-coats" to Calum. We tiptoed back to the chopping block, dropped the axe, picked up his sack and blanket and walked with speed and silence into the forest. We both knew from cattle raids that surprise was the best weapon. We knew they were there, they did not know we were leaving. Fleeing too fast would make noise, alerting the Redcoats to our escape.

We moved through the brush and then the trees as quick and quiet as hares. It was difficult to keep our emotions under control, especially when we heard the Redcoats calling to each other as the searched for us. The sleepy feeling from the sweets made it even tougher to concentrate on fleeing. We did not speak, did not pause for at least an hour when the sun set.

"The red blanket in the window," Calum said, panting with the effort of our escape.

"What?" I asked, trying to recover my breath.

"The old woman hung a red blanket in the window when we got there. She said it was to keep the chill out but it must have been a signal. When Redcoats are in the area and see a red blanket in the window, they know someone they are looking for is inside."

"She was turning us over to the Redcoats." I sat down on the ground.

"They take care of her but I doubt any of them is her son."

Whatever had made us tired at the old woman's house did not leave us for a full day. We walked that full second day to make sure the Redcoats did not catch up with us but it was at a much slower pace.

The daily snow showers turned to rain and sleet. Searching for Redcoats, fighting the weather, the tired feeling, my illness and constant hunger slowed our progress toward Greenock.

My fever began to improve. If it had been spring, I would have found some thyme and licorice growing along our path. Chewing on thyme leaves soothes a sore throat. Licorice eases body aches. My fever would have been gone in a day or so. But it was winter and the herbs were buried under ground. After what happened with the old woman, we were too afraid to approach anyone else to find a healer. We ventured into villages to steal food from windowsills. The MacIain had taught us that it was okay to borrow without asking as long as there was a good reason. I was ill for many days and to me, that was a good reason.

"I think we should go back," I said. "To the glen." I added.

"We cannot."

"Why not? The best healers in the world are in the glen. The weather is getting warmer. It will be easier to travel back than it has been to get here."

"We are almost there, Dory. You have to accept that you are going."

Why was he being difficult? Did he not understand how much I wanted to go back?

"It's better for the clan if I stay."

"Dory, do you understand why your father and uncle are sending you to the New World?"

"Because they fear for my life. They should know I am just as willing to die for the clan as they are. I grew up listening to the great battles of our ancestors spilling blood to protect life in the glen. My duty is to the MacDonalds of Glencoe."

Power soared through me as I spoke and I did not want to walk at Calum's pace anymore. I took the lead on our journey. Calum walked faster to keep up with me but let me pick the way.

"Exactly," Calum said. "That is why you have to go. Your duty to the clan."

"That makes no sense."

"If the king sends someone to finish what Glenlyon started, the clan will be wiped out. It is clear that was his intent and who can stop him? You are the best chance for the survival of the clan. Your father and the chief believe you will survive the journey across the ocean." He slipped and struggled to keep his feet as I continued to stomp at a fast pace. "You are also well versed in clan tradition and are clever enough to find a way to observe them and teach new generations, your children. If the king succeeds in killing off the clan in Scotland, we will live through you in the New World."

I was silent. Stunned. I thought being sent away was a show of how weak I was but Calum was saying the opposite. Could he be right? Why would John not have told me?

"Look, even if the clan does survive in Scotland, everything is different in the glen now. Gilbert is gone, your mother is gone, and your grandfather is gone. Death is not new to us, but so much death at once from a dishonorable ambush is something we have never dealt with before. Your father and the chief are right. The New World will be a big change for you, but so would going back to the glen. Nothing will be the same for any of us."

For the first time I thought about Calum's situation. His father and older brothers were killed in a skirmish over cattle a few years back, his sister had married and headed north with her husband from Ross. His mother most likely had been a victim of Glenlyon's men. Yet, here he was, skulking through the Scottish wilderness to get me to Greenock because he believed in the power of our clan. Perhaps he was not as weak minded as I thought.

I walked faster and faster, pounding my feet on the ground with every step.

BOOM!

I stopped walking. Calum stopped, too. "What was that?" I asked.

Cre-e-e-ea-k-k-k!

"The ice!!" Calum shrieked. "The ice is breaking!"

"What ice?"

I looked down. In my surge of power, I had led us to the middle of a frozen loch.

Cra-a-a-aaa-ck-ck-k!

It sounded like a creature was breaking its way up to the surface.

Under my feet, spreading out in all directions were huge cracks grow-ing larger and longer as I stood staring at them.

Calum panicked. He turned to run back to solid ground. His back foot broke through the ice. Off balance, he threw his arms in the air, sending his sack falling to the ice. I lay on my belly so if a hole appeared I would not bob into it like a cork that never rises to the surface. Calum managed to keep himself from falling through the ice and scur-ried back to the banks with little more than a wet foot and a lost sack. I crawled on my belly at a slow, agonizing pace. I reached the sack and slid it to the edge of the loch. A couple of things fell into the hole in the ice made by Calum's foot.

The minutes passed like hours as I tried to escape the breaking ice. Panting and scared, I arrived at the banks of the loch. My clothes were wet from the inside because I was sweating and from the outside from the watery ice. Even though the weather had begun to warm, it was still very cold. Sitting on the edge of the loch, soaked from the inside out I was cold and tired. I needed to sit there for a while. Calum was sitting and panting as well.

"That was close," he said as I tried to catch my breath. My chest hurt and I started coughing. "The weather must have gotten warm enough to start melting the ice."

"It sounded like a kelpie was coming up at me," I managed to get out.

"A kelpie, Dory? It was the sun."

"You were not out as far as I was. You did not see everything."

"Did you see a horse under the water?"

"No. Do you not believe in kelpies either? What do you believe in?"

"The clan." He picked up his things. "Do you want to get to the other side of the loch or camp here for the night?"

Damp, cold, tired, hungry and with labored breath, I considered his question.

"We will have to hike all the way around the loch since we cannae go over it. Camping back from the edge a bit makes the most sense."

It was a few minutes later, after we had found a good spot to camp, that Calum started to make the fire. He looked in his sack.

"Uh, oh," he whispered. "The flint."

"What?" I asked. I was busy with the blankets. "What did you say?"

"The flint. It's gone."

I stared at him. "The flint is gone? How are we going make a fire without flint?"

"We? I always make the fire."

"Fine. Now that *you* lost the flint, how will *you* make the fire?"

"*I* lost the flint? You are the one who flung the sack around the ice and let the flint fall into the hole."

"A hole you made! I slid the sack because you dropped it."

"Whatever. We need to find another way to make a fire."

"Another way? There is no other way. No one else is around to get fire from, the flint is gone, we are going to freeze in our sleep and the legacy of the Glencoe MacDonalds will die with us."

"There has to be something. Look around. Are there any rocks that look like they might work?"

It was, of course, a ridiculous idea but we searched anyway. Nothing.

"What about your sacks? Is there anything in them that might work?"

"Like what?" I asked as I opened the first sack. "Oats? No, I do not think they will make a flame. The stone in the bottom would break if you hit against the dagger." I opened the second. "The coins? There is no flint in coins, Calum."

"What's in the third?" he asked.

"Nothing. It had my mother's necklace in it but now it's empty." Without thinking, my hand shot up to my throat to make sure my mother's cairngorm was around my neck. It was secure in its spot. "Wait! I put the elf-bolt in the sack. Maybe that will work!"

"Elf-bolt?" Calum asked. "How is that going to help us?"

"Because elves made it which means it has powers, that's how." I did not wait to listen to him tell me that he did not believe in elves either. I knelt down, picked up the dagger and struck the elf-bolt against it. Over and over, strike after strike, I hit the small pointed rock against the steel dagger. I hoped it would work. Then the kindling glowed.

"I don't believe it," Calum said.

I blew on the kindling and added a few twigs. Soon there was a small fire. Merlin appeared on a nearby tree limb. I did not try to hide my smile.

"Believe it," I said. "We have been saved by elves."

Chapter Twelve

The smile on my face was pure joy. I knew it annoyed Calum but I did not care. He was sure that dealing with the supernatural was dangerous. Mother had told me that a little wicked goes a long way and I believed that to be true. But this was not wicked or evil. This was using what was necessary to get the job done. Plain and simple.

After drying off and getting a bite of oatmeal, I decided not to mention the elf-bolt to Calum again. He had to use it every time we made a fire for the rest of our trip and that would be satisfaction enough.

"Do you know where we are?" I asked a few days later. We had been walking for days without saying much. I was thinking about my new role in the clan. Who knew what thoughts were roaming around in Calum's head.

"We must be near one of the smaller lochs by Loch Lomond, I think." Calum pointed down the loch. "There's an abandoned Campbell castle south of here. My father told us about it when it was destroyed."

We were both quiet again. I was thinking about all that the Campbells had taken from me. I guessed that Calum was thinking the same.

"Do you think we can make it?" I asked.

"Make what?"

"Make it to the castle before it is too dark to see the next step in front of us?"

"It is a castle no longer, Dory. Do you not see? It has been attacked, the walls toppled, the insides burned beyond use. That is why it is abandoned."

"Exactly."

I picked up the pace and Calum was quick to keep up with me, although he still did not understand my thinking.

"Why do we want to make it to the castle ruin?"

"Walls," I explained. "Most of the walls were toppled but there must still be parts of some remaining. When a castle is destroyed, the attacker demolishes it to the point where it would take too much money and man power to rebuild, at least while war was still raging. There is no need to raze it to the ground. You can see parts of it sticking up from here. There is bound to be a little part still standing a few feet, from the ground to where the last rock was blown off by the enemy. Behind that little wall, we can build a fire that need not fight wind on all sides. If we are lucky, there may be a mossy bit to sit or sleep on up against the wall instead of the cold hard ground and patches of icy snow we have had so far. There is a chance for comfort in that castle, even though it is a ruin."

Calum said nothing. I did not know if he thought me mad talking about a ruin as a comfortable place to spend the night or if he was embarrassed that he had not been the one to suggest it.

The closer we got to the castle, the more we could see that I was right. Here and there, bits of castle wall stood above the ground with no supporting walls around it, like an outcropping of heather. The sights quickened my pace once more. I was determined that we would have a better night's rest. We crossed the threshold of the once proud building while the sky was enjoying the last dimming light of the day. I searched as best I could in the darkening cold air while Calum swore with every stumble.

"Can we just rest here?" he whined. "My belly aches for oatcakes."

"My back aches for a good stretch-out."

Just then, I reached the part of the ruin that was not torn down to the ground and there it stood. Oh, it was more glorious than I had hoped. A corner! Two small walls still connected at the edge. One wall was at least as long as Calum lying down and almost half as high. A fine fire could roar there, laughing at the howling wind. I ventured a bit further and peeked out over the edge. There, about two feet from the ground, built into the wall was a long bench made of one piece of carved stone. It had to have been a window seat. Perhaps some lovely lady had sat at this seat to weave or stitch as she watched her wee ones play in the courtyard. It would have been a homey scene, until the day someone destroyed her home in a violent rage and killed her kinfolk. Campbell or not, I felt the lady's pain.

Calum arrived at our new little corner and got to work building a fire without saying a word. I set to my chores as well, setting out supplies to fix the ache in Calum's belly. Pride in my castle-ruin find kept my spirits high and I found it difficult to keep myself from humming. How odd the destruction of a home could bring us such good fortune.

"Do you think we will have company tonight?"

"We have not seen a soul for two days. You worry too much," I said.

"The chief gave me an important job and I will not be the one to let down the clan. I cannae worry too much."

I did not want to think about his duty or his worries so I busied myself with cooking and hiding the supplies from animals who might be in the area. Red foxes, most likely, who would not be eager to attempt climbing very high.

After the fire, roaring compared to recent standards, had burned long enough to warm the air around it, I laid my blanket on the ground and wrapped my plaid around myself. I smiled as my eyes closed, ready for a wonderful sleep.

I woke confused, unable to understand the strange sensation. I was cold but not like normal. The fire was still going, Calum must have added to it or it would have faded. I looked over to see that he had fallen asleep. Normally we took shifts, one slept as well as possible while the other tended the fire and kept alert for unusual sounds that might be animals or enemies approaching. Napping during guard duty would never be tolerated in the glen but on the run, sometimes it could not be helped. Instead of waking him to finish his shift, I decided to stay awake for a bit and see if he woke on his own.

The coldness came back, a shiver that zinged up my spine and left through my hair. My hair moved as the coldness ran through it. I would not mention it to Calum as he did not believe in wraiths. I spent the rest of the night thinking about what kind of wraith it might have been. That is, until I feel asleep.

It was the best night's sleep we had had since the attack.

"We are a few days from Greenock," Calum said after our breakfast. "Are you ready to get on a ship when we get there?"

Now that I understood why the clan leaders had chosen me to go to the New World, I would go willingly. No side trips to Edinburgh to find my father. The MacDonalds of Glencoe could not be forgotten. I had to make sure.

"Aye," I said. "I will not bother you anymore about turning back."

In a few days' time, we reached the edge of a large body of water where Loch Long flows into the Firth of Clyde. On the other side was Greenock. The currents were strong. We could not cross the waters alone. We needed a boat. I considered stealing one but there were too many people around. We would have to pay for our passage.

The first few boatmen we saw were not at all friendly. They were tying knots, gutting fish or yelling at younger men who were doing most of the work. We found one man who seemed quiet. I paid him two coins to allow Calum and me to cross the water with him.

After we docked, we thanked the man and headed in the direction of Greenock. Two mornings later, we started our last day together. I pulled the elf-bolt sack off the leather strap and handed it to Calum.

"You will need this to get back," I said.

"Thanks." We did not talk about how the fires were much quicker to get started with the elf-bolt than with the flint we lost. I knew why but Calum would not agree.

"We should split the oats and money, too." I suggested.

"I will take some of the oats but you will need the money."

We agreed to split the oats in half. It amazed me how long the oats had lasted. I was going to leave my family's stone in my sack but thought of how mother would whisper to it now and again. Perhaps the stone was what kept the sack full. Calum would need more oats for his journey since I would be on a ship and even if he did not believe in the supernatural, maybe it could help him from starving anyway. I dropped the stone is his sack along with more than a few coins, just to make sure he could pay someone if he needed help. We had one water jug and decided that Calum should take it. I gave him the leather strap as well and tucked the one sack I had left under my skirt.

The deal done, we set out on our final walk. I wanted to thank Calum for risking his life to get me to Greenock and for explaining why I had to go to the New World. What could I say, though? We walked in silence as we had done most of our time together. I decided to thank him at the docks before I boarded the ship. An hour or two into our journey we heard voices from behind us. The sounds did not concern me at first, there were towns nearby the woods in which we were walking. Then voices got louder and we could hear what they were saying.

"This way," one said. "The old man said they were headed toward Greenock."

"The old man?" I whispered. "The guy who took us across the firth must have told on us. We told him nothing. I even spoke to him in Scots. How could he know where we were from or where we were going?"

"No matter now," Calum said. "We have to leave the woods to get to the ships. We will have to run for it."

I looked outside the tree line to the open field outside the wooded area. There were a few yards of open grass and then the town popped up. It was a busy place with people moving about, ships being loaded and unloaded, merchants buying and selling right off the ships, passengers exchanging teary good-byes with those staying in Scotland.

"Ready," I said.

The second we left the cover of the trees, the first shot fired out. It exploded in a tree less than a yard away.

"Go back!" I yelled to Calum. "If we stay together, they will get one of us!"

"Good luck, Dory!" he yelled. "Be careful!"

"Thank you!"

He turned back to the soldiers in their red coats and yelled, "Hey, you ugly tailed dogs, here I am!" He disappeared behind a tree just as the guns fired.

I took off in the direction of the ship docks. Out of the corner of my eye, I saw a brown creature flying near me. Merlin! He was following me to the docks.

Do not lose me now!

I tried to disappear in the first crowd I saw as Calum had with the trees. I hoped Calum had made it into the full cover of the forest without injury. If he could get back to the woods, he might be able to hide from the Redcoats. It seemed to me that most of the soldiers had followed me into the crowd. I went up to a man who looked like he was in charge. I had heard a sailor call him 'captain.'

"Excuse me sir," I said with wheezy breaths. Since my illness with the fever, my breath was quick to leave me. "Are you going to America?"

"Spain," he said shaking his head. "What part of the colonies you headed to?"

"The area settled by the Massachusetts Bay Company," I said, hoping I pronounced it correctly.

"Lots of ships goin' there. Do you know what port you're wantin'?"

I thought for a moment, anxious to remember what Mother had told me about my aunt. Were they in Boston? No, it was a port smaller than Boston. Or was it north of Boston? Both?

"North of Boston," I said, hoping I was right.

"Then you're wantin' to see Captain Harris. Third ship down the way, there. It's a cargo ship but he takes on a few passengers if he has room. The captain wears a yellow felt hat. Be careful, though, lass. He can be an awful grouch."

"Aye, thank you, sir." I glanced over my shoulder to see if the soldiers had found me. I did not know how good a look at me any of them got. Many of the people on the docks looked as dirty and desperate as I must have. It was easy to find the ship the first captain had described. There were not many men with wide-brimmed yellow felt hats.

"I need passage to Massachusetts Bay colony," I blurted out.

"Why would I take such a rude, dirty little lass to America on my ship?" he asked. The captain was dressed in a red and white striped shirt, mustard yellow waistcoat and red pants. His shoes had large rusty buckles. His clothes looked worn at the elbows and knees.

"Pardon me, Captain Harris, sir," I said, remembering my manners. "I need to get to my uncle. He lives in a port city north of Boston and will be able to pay my fare when we arrive."

"And if he can not?"

Good question. "I will work off my fare."

"A tiny little girl like you? What could you do?"

"I can cook and clean."

He laughed a mean chortle. "A Scottish lass who claims she can cook? You will not find many people in the New World willing to eat your haggis. You do not look sturdy enough to clean anything heavier a spider web."

"I am strong, sir. And I can cook more than haggis." He had to agree to take me. The soldiers were closing in.

"Aye, I am going to a port north of Boston. That stone around your neck must be worth something. Not enough for the whole fare, though. I will hold it until your debt is paid."

No, not my mother's necklace. I could never take it off.

"This stone is worth nothing. I found it in a loch at home. I would not want to deceive you, sir."

Merlin perched on the ropes used to load cargo onto the ship. He appeared to be guarding my necklace.

"You know that bird?"

I did not know what to say. If the captain liked birds, Merlin could help me get on the ship but if he hated them, I would never get on.

A bright colored bird flew from the deck and landed on Captain Harris's shoulder.

"Stupid bird," the captain muttered. "This thing never shuts its beak. All day and all night, I can hear this thing squawking. And all it says is 'stupid bird.'"

Awwk! Awwk! Merlin called down. The parrot on the captain's shoulder crawled to the other shoulder, putting the captain's head between himself and Merlin.

"What is this?" the captain asked. "That bird got this stupid parrot to be quiet."

"It seems your parrot may be afraid of my Merlin."

"Your Merlin is it? I won this stupid bird from a pirate near Barbados. Turns out he lost it to me on purpose."

"Why not sell him or set him free?" I asked.

"I am keeping this bird until one of us dies or I get my revenge on that pirate by losing this bird back to him."

Not a great plan. Even if he could find the pirate, why would he play for the bird he lost on purpose? I decided not to point that out to Captain Harris.

The parrot started bobbing his head. Merlin opened his wings and folded them again. He rested his weight on his left leg. The parrot stopped.

"Amazing," the captain said. "What's your name, lass?"

"Dory."

"Well, Dory, I will take you and your bird to the Massachusetts Bay colony and we will find your uncle and see if he will pay your fare. If not, you will cook and scrub for my wife there until I say your debt is paid. But, you have to prove that is your bird."

"Fine," I said. I hoped Merlin could understand how important it was that he obey me. I held out my arm. "Come, Merlin!"

He paused for a moment and then took flight. He circled the ship then flew down toward me. Since I did not have my leather glove to protect my skin from his talons, I dropped my arm as he approached. Merlin landed on the dock beside me. I smiled with utter relief and silently thanked both Merlin and Gilbert.

Captain Harris clapped. "Excellent! We have a deal, then?"

I could see this was not an honorable man and he might never let me out of the contract. What choice did I have?

"Aye, sir."

The Captain walked with me to a small house near the dock used for business. Inside, a man dressed in all green sat behind a desk with a large ledger. A gold chain held his spectacles. The man greeted the captain who told him our terms. The man's bluish-black ink stained fingers worked fast writing out the contract. Captain Harris read it over and then signed it.

"Sign here," the man said. As soon as I signed the contract, the captain would have legal authority over me. Not even my uncle would have the power to save me. I could not just take his word for what was in the contract.

"Sir, could you read it to me?" I asked the man dressed in green.

"Read it?" he asked.

"Aye, sir. I want to make sure I understand it before I sign it."

"This one understands business, Hank," Captain Harris said. He had a strange look on his face. Was it annoyance or pride? "Go ahead and read it to her. She has a right to know what she is signing."

The businessman, Hank, shrugged and read the contract aloud. It sounded right. When he finished reading, I put my 'X' where he told me. I had to trust the contract said what the captain had dictated and the man had read.

Captain Harris clapped his hand on my shoulder.

"Welcome aboard the Raven, lass!"

Captain Harris told me that since I had not paid yet I could not travel with the paying passengers. He had another idea.

"You will be the bird caretaker," he said, "and travel with the animals. Of course, that makes you part of the crew. Men do not like a lass on their crew."

"I work hard," I promised.

"It is not a matter of effort. A lass alone among men is not a good idea, ever. You need some breeks and a long shirt."

"You want me to pretend to be a boy?"

"Not to worry. It will be safe. You will bed down with the animals."

Living among the animals would be fine with me. That was how we lived in the glen. But pretending to be a boy for the whole trip across the ocean? How would I do that?

"I have no money to buy new clothes," I said.

"You have wits, though, don't, ya?" He smiled at me. "We finish loading in one hour. You and your bird should be onboard by then."

Chapter Thirteen

There was no time to think. I had signed a contract and was indebted to the Captain. I had to do as he said and find a way to look like a boy so I could cross the ocean on his ship. I looked around the bustling neighborhood, trying to figure out how to find new clothes in less than an hour. MacIain's borrowing without asking rule applied here again just as when Calum and I had stolen a few bites to eat on our journey. The problem was figuring out where to find some unattended clothes.

The best option was a wash line. I walked through the alley by the business house and down a few more until I found laundry hanging behind three homes. I looked around to make sure no one was in the alley. Then I eyed the clothing on the three lines. After a few tries I had clothes fit for a servant boy. I ducked inside one of the outhouses.

Peeling off the clothes I had worn since the attack in the glen was painful. The fabric seemed to cling to me, tugging on my skin as I pulled it away, like my soul trying to cling to Scotland itself. There were no stockings on the lines, which meant I had to keep my own on, rips, tears, dirt and all. The shirt was too large, falling below my knees but the blue waistcoat fit okay. It was lucky that my chest was as flat as a boy's was. I buttoned the shirt to cover my mother's necklace. It was the one thing I had to keep, besides Merlin, and the fewer people who saw it, the better. Pulling on the breeks was strange. There was so much material. The shirt and pants bunched together in awkward places. It was uncomfortable. Satisfied that I looked like a boy, I peeked out before emerging from the outhouse. The alley was still empty of people.

My broken heart ached as I wrapped the tatters of my highland clothes in my plaid. The temptation to keep them was strong but the Redcoats were searching the streets for any flash of a highland tartan. I dropped my bundle under the line as if it had fallen there and walked toward the alley. Tears stung my eyes and stuck my hair to my face. My hair! I had to have something to hold my hair back. I had a great idea what to use. Glancing around to make sure I was still alone, I ran back to the bundle of clothes and ripped off the hem of my skirt. It was so dirty and worn that the tartan pattern could not be seen but I knew it was there. The only scrap of fabric from my home would hold my hair back in the braid of a boy servant.

"Okay, Merlin," I said. He was perched in a tree. "Now we need a hat." Merlin took off, spreading his beautiful wings. He circled a block a few times and then dove out of sight. It was how he acted when he saw a skylark. I ran to the area where Merlin had flown. Soon he appeared above the tops of the houses. There was something red in his beak. It was a Monmouth cap! Had he stolen it off someone's head? I had meant to buy a cap with the few coins I had and maybe a scrap of bread to quiet my stomach. Changing direction away from the shops, I headed back to the ship. Merlin flew ahead and I saw him land on the same rigging ropes where he had perched earlier.

"You, there!" a voice called toward me. I did not turn to see who was yelling. It was probably the man whose cap Merlin had stolen. "I order you to stop!" Order? I looked over my shoulder and saw a Redcoat yelling to me. Before I could figure out what to do, I slammed cheek-first into another Redcoat whose belly was round but not squishy.

"Where are you off to lad?" he asked, grabbing hold of my upper arm. At least he thought I was a lad. The first soldier caught up to us.

"Was it you who had his hat stolen by that mangy bird?"

Mangy bird? How dare he say that about Merlin?

"You mute, boy?" the fat one asked pulling hard on my arm and squeezing it tighter. It hurt so much I thought I would cry. Again.

"Non, monsieur." For some reason, French seemed like the best choice.

"Was it your cap that was stolen?"

"Non, monsieur."

"Then why were you running?"

"Non, monsieur." I hoped that if they thought I did not understand them, they would let me go. It worked.

"He does not know anything, Ted. Keep looking." The fat one released my arm.

I took off for the ship, running as fast as I could in my new awkward clothes. My knees kept catching on the extra fabric. I stumbled a few times but managed not to fall.

Captain Harris was waiting on the ship as I ran up the gangplank. He had a bemused look on his face as Merlin dropped the cap. I picked up the round woven wool cap and pulled it on my head. It was too big and fell over my eyes. I pushed it up in order to see.

"You do make an entrance," he said. The captain turned to the closest worker, a tall skinny man in mismatched clothing. "Gerry, take our new recruit to the animals' quarters."

"Aye, Cap'n."

Gerry put down the crate he was carrying on a stack of other crates and started walking in the opposite direction without a word to me. I followed him. Men were everywhere, some were stacking and moving cargo and others removing the ropes that tethered the ship to the dock. It was not until Gerry led me to the top of a set of wooden stairs that I realized we were no longer attached to Scotland.

It would take hours, many hours before there was not a speck of land to be seen from any part of the ship. I wanted to stand on deck and stare and stare until I thought my eyes would bulge out of my head. Smaller and smaller, the strip of land would shrink as my hope of seeing my father or uncle standing on shore demanding my safe return shrank with it. I wanted to watch the sun move from one side of the sky to the other at an agonizing pace until the final dot disappeared from view, when even the final shadow of the last rock would no longer be visible to me. I could not, of course. I had too much to learn about life on a ship. My beaten but still beating heart sank a bit lower in my chest.

My Scotland was gone from me forever and I from it. I was drifting, alone and scared, in the middle of the great, wide, deep ocean.

Chapter Fourteen

Clouds moved to cover the sun. The darkened sky matched my mood. I had to remind myself that Father and the chief thought sending me to the New World would help preserve the traditions of the MacDonalds of Glencoe. Mother wanted this voyage for me as well. She had to have believed that her sister would recognize the necklace and claim me as her kin. I had nothing to do but accept my fate and prepare for the ocean crossing.

Gerry, as it turned out, was in charge of the goats and sheep on board. I was in charge of the parrot and Merlin.

"Never had a bird boy before," Gerry said. "When we got chickens on board, I take care of them. Them chickens is loud. Glad we don't have none this time."

"Ahh." I did not want to say too much in case he thought I sounded like a girl. Plus he smelled like he had already been at sea for a month.

"Passengers make their own food. Guess you eat in the forecastle with us. Food is part of our pay but not much. They feed us just enough to keep us from keeling over."

"Aye." We descended the stairs one deck below the main and were getting closer to the animals. The smells of hay and animal farts were thick. A twinge of homesickness rippled through my body.

"Crew don't get much meat," he said. "Duff and oatmeal porridge mostly."

Great. More oatmeal.

"Best things really," Gerry continued. "It's why passengers are puking in rough seas and crew don't. Our stomachs is better off. You ain't been on a crew before, huh?"

Being found out by the first person who talked to me that I had never been on a crew was not a good sign. I had better learn more about this ship.

I shrugged. "Work where I can."

"Right, right. Captain Harris is okay. Just don't go near him when he's in one of his moods. Mean as a three-legged goat."

I had never seen a three-legged goat but it sounded mean. I nodded.

"Captain says you'll stay down here. Don't know why, not my business. Just stay clear of the passengers. Some of them bunk on the other side of that blanket. The goats and sheep ain't a bother so long as their food holds out. Don't know what the birds eat. I gotta get back to the forecastle. My watch is in four hours. See ya."

I gave a weird little wave by way of acknowledging him. He must have thought I was a strange lad but again, at least he thought I was a boy.

Gerry had left me in a small area made smaller by food crates, casks of beer and wine, barrels, sacks, trunks, chests, bedrolls, and of course, the animals. Squirming to find more room, the sheep shuffled their hooves and the goats made a strange noise from their throats. Only a thin blanket hung between the area for passengers and the one for the animals and me.

The reality of my new situation weighed on me. I had to learn how the ship worked and at the same time stay out of sight as much as possible. I also had to corral two birds, one who I knew would disobey me whenever he wanted and the other of whom I knew nothing.

Merlin had stayed above deck. I hoped he was keeping out of trouble. The Captain's parrot was on his shoulder last I saw. With the birds in my charge out of the cargo hold, I decided to explore my new home for the next few months. It was better than wondering if Calum had escaped the Redcoats and if he knew that my hurried 'thank you' had been for more than his wish of good luck. True to Scottish weather, which could change in seconds, when I emerged on the top deck the sun almost knocked me over.

Men were pulling ropes, mopping the deck, yelling at each other. I had to keep moving, even though I was unsure where to go. Standing still while everyone else was working seemed dangerous. Someone might see you and give you a job. Since I had no idea how to do any of these things, I tried to look as busy as possible.

Walking toward the back of the ship, what the sailors called the 'aft,' I climbed a small set of five or six stairs to the highest part of the ship. A door squeaked on its hinges and a huge fluff of color burst toward me.

Rah! Stupid bird! Rah!

"Stupid parrot!" Captain Harris stormed out the same door. When he saw me, he smirked. "Dory! It's about time!" He disappeared behind the door again.

Stupid Bird landed on my shoulder. Before I could shoo him off the captain came back carrying a group of twigs twisted together into a crude cage.

"Here's his cage and there's a sack of seeds in the cargo hold. He eats whatever fruit you might get, if you do. Keep him away from me or you will find out why punishment at sea is known as the most severe in the world." He disappeared back into his cabin, slamming the door behind him.

Rah! Stupid bird! Rah!

Stunned and feeling the pinch of the parrot's claws on my shoulder, I stood still, crude cage in hand. I had no idea what to do next. The one thing I knew for sure was that I had to get away from the Captain's quarters before Stupid Bird could squawk again. I took the steps two at a time and headed back to my cargo hold. Fixing the cage would be a good step, if I could make it strong enough to hold the bird.

Chapter Fifteen

Before ever being aboard one, to my thinking, the great ships that crossed the Atlantic were floating fortresses, but made of wood instead of brick and stone. Once on the Raven, I realized how small it was. There was no courtyard to grab a breath of fresh air, no large dining table for the men to share a meal, no armory to store stocks of weapons. The truth was, there was no fresh air to catch, no time to linger over conversation at a meal and no stock of weapons that I could see. If pirates or anyone else attacked the Raven, once the few cannonballs were gone it would be every man and Bird Boy for himself. I wondered if the passengers knew that.

The Raven, as ships go, was good enough. The wide planks that served as flooring for each deck had been laid long ago and had seen enough seawater, swabbing buckets and storms to have warped. Some were split and separated at points but for the most part one could go from one end of the ship to the other without fear of finding oneself crashing through to the deck below. The outer planks had the tight seals of a new ship, of course, or we never would have made it out of the firth and into the ocean. As I walked the ship, I listened to the constant creaks. It reminded me of the constant coughing of our people back home. It was a strange comfort but any comfort at sea is a good one.

Chores were abundant. Everywhere I went men were sewing sails, cleaning everything from scrubbing and swabbing the deck to shining brass bells and other instruments. The only thing in need of a good scrubbing on the Raven was her crew. Oh how the men stunk. In the glen, a man would wash in the River Coe at least once a week and had a good warm bath two or three times a year like a civilized creature!

I wondered if the chores were necessary to keep the ship working or if they were a way to keep the men busy for months at sea. Gambling occurred, mainly a strange dice game that seemed to favor the more experienced men, but I did not witness any violent outbreaks because of this activity. Perhaps the punishment for violence was enough to keep the men's tempers in check.

When the crewmembers glared at the 'bird boy,' it was creepy. I was grateful that the captain had made me dress as a lad. Even the paying women passengers never went near the crew. These were sea-faring men who were interested in surviving the dangerous trip across the ocean to collect their pay. To them my chores were easy, take care of two small birds and help with the cooking. They, on the other hand, were constantly cleaning, tying ropes, unfurling and closing sails, maintaining all the equipment for the next watch to use. The one crewmember who did not scowl at me was an older man, Horace. He was the main navigator. I took to spending my time in steerage when I could.

"Back again, I see," Horace said when I came into the small room with no windows.

"Aye, sir."

A table took up most of the space and held equipment including a large map with markings on it. Stupid Bird perched on the door since he could not fit on my shoulder in the cramped space.

It was also a good place to learn about the ship and how it worked. Hanging on the wall was a wooden board. Horace called it a traverse board. A 32-point rose compass was painted on the rounded part of the board with holes punched at each point. Tied to the center of the board by small ropes were eight wooden pegs. Every half-hour, a sailor looked at the ship's compass and put a peg in a hole to show the direction of the ship. The board had eight columns of holes for each of the 32 rose-points, enough to track the ship every thirty minutes for a four-hour watch.

Two crewmembers came to the room, took a few pieces of equipment and left.

"Go help Charles and Ephram with the line," Horace instructed. "It is Monday, after all."

"Aye, sir."

I had no idea what Monday had to do with anything but I headed outside anyway. The wind was picking up. I pulled my wool cap down around my ears and pushed it up above my eyes. Stupid Bird flew to my shoulder.

"Why do you wear boots?" Ephram asked. It was so seldom that anyone spoke to me that it took a moment to realize he meant my boots.

"It's all I got." Sticking as close to the truth as possible was essential while telling a lie. The highland leather boots were all that I had, worn through in spots from my journey with Calum. There had been no shoes on the clothesline.

The two looked at each other and shrugged. Charles handed me a wooden dowel with weights tied to it.

"Throw this off when I say so," he said. "When I say stop, you grab the rope before any more of it crosses the railing. Can you handle that? Or should I have the bird do it?"

As far as insults go, that was tame. I let it go. I had no idea what we were doing but Horace had told me to help them. As I walked to the aft railing, Charles stuck his foot in my way and tripped me. I hit the wooden deck hard, chin-first. I had not let go of the dowel because I did not know how fragile it was or if the ship had another one if I broke this one. Blood trickled out my mouth from where I bit through the edge of my lip but I said nothing. The punishment I would have suffered if the instrument had broken would have been much worse I was sure. A bloody lip was getting off easy.

"Looks like those boots are a hazard," Charles said. He and Ephram laughed. Not a full-bellied Henderson lad laugh like when they teased me in the glen, but the meaning was the same. They had power over me and wanted me to know it. That was fine. There was nothing I could do about it. For now.

I stood up and took my place at the railing.

"Go!" he yelled. I tossed the dowel behind the ship. Charles turned over the sandglass and watched the sand fall from the top to the bottom.

Rope spun off the spool in Ephram's hands.

"Stop!" he yelled.

As soon as my hands touched the unspooling rope, splinters bit into my palms. Resisting the urge to pull my hand back, I grabbed the rope and pulled until the weighted dowel, now wet, was once again in my hand.

"Three and a half," Charles said.

"Aye, three and a half," Ephram repeated. I had so many questions. As if reading my mind he began to explain. "Gerry said you never been on a crew before, not that you are now. Well, bird boy, the rope is knotted at even intervals. We count how many knots go over the railing in the time it takes the sandglass to run out. That is how fast the ship is moving. This time we stopped the rope between the third and fourth knot. We call it three and a half."

"What are you doing?" Charles asked his crewmate.

Ephram shrugged. "Monday."

That was twice. What did Monday have to do with anything? How did the day of the week possible matter out in the middle of the ocean?

"Fine," Charles said. Turning to me, he continued. "Back in steerage, we use the four rows of holes at the bottom of the traverse board to record the number of knots."

I knew I was risking more teasing and physical harm but I had to ask.

"Why does Monday matter?"

"Oh, the bird boy asks questions, now, eh?" Charles said.

"Mondays are training days. Every Monday crewmembers try to

learn new skills. You should think of everyday as Monday."

Charles and Ephram thought this a brilliant and funny idea. They laughed a bit more hardy this time. They returned the equipment to Horace's room and made their marks on the traverse board. I realized how young they were. Not much older than young Ian Henderson. I wondered what made them leave their homes at such a young age. Who were they running from? Perhaps they were just as scared and uncertain about what would happen to them as I was.

I bit at the rope splinters in my hand. Horace glanced at the blood on my face and smiled.

News of my injury on the aft deck spread throughout the ship. Crewmembers went out of their way to cross my path in order to punch, trip or shove me. One night, I slipped up to the top deck to check on Merlin. He was leaning on his left leg, sound asleep on the ropes.

I was about to go back down without being seen when Stupid Bird gave me away.

Rah! Stupid Bird! Rah!

Ephram, who had been asleep at his post, did not like being awakened by the parrot. He grabbed me by the arm before I could get away. Stupid Bird flew off my shoulder. Traitor.

Ephram punched me in the stomach, sending me to my knees, gasping for breath

"Shut that bird up," he growled in my ear.

He sauntered off, proud of beating on a weaker crewmember. I stayed frozen until he was gone. Being the newest member of the crew, not having the same workload as the rest and being smaller than everyone else made me the perfect target. I took all their abuse as best I could. Earning respect from these men was important but that would not stop them from beating on me just because they could. At home in the glen, I was protected from pranks to an extent because my grandfather was the chief. On the Raven, I had no position.

The passengers looked down on me because they thought I was part of the crew. They were more insulted by having to sleep near me than the animals. The crew looked down on me because all I had to do was take care of two birds. I belonged nowhere. Not one of the crew, not even Gerry, talked to me unless it was to set me up for a trip or punch. I was on a ship of over a hundred people and the only one that talked to me was Stupid Bird. My homesickness grew more intense every day and my heart grew heavier every time I thought of my family. I wondered about Calum and if he made it back to Glencoe. I prayed that my father was safe, wherever he was. I tried to imagine them both back home in our burned out baile. I wished with all my reconstructed-yet-broken heart that I were back there, too.

The crew ate in a part of the ship called the forecastle. It was nothing like any castle I had ever seen. Located at the front of the ship, it held the bunks for the crew and their belongings, food and a place for a small cook fire. Crates, barrels and chests cramped the space, there were no windows and it smelled of unwashed men. I stayed long enough to help the cabin boys and the cook. Although flour, beef fat and raisins boiled in a sack, which the sailors called 'duff' could hardly be called a meal. Most of the crew relied on the daily rations of beer for nourishment.

It was easy to tell which men had spent a life at sea and which were new to the profession. It was not because of the speed or confidence with which they performed their tasks, as some of the new men had a great deal of enthusiasm for their adventure and the more experienced had already done these things thousands of times over and no longer found joy in them. The difference was in how they looked. Not just age but how they had aged. Old-timers had deep lines and creases around their eyes, eyes that were in a permanent squint position. Crusty bits from the constant salt in the air lodged in these creases, changing their appearance even more. Men new to the sea would try to shield their eyes from glaring sun rays as they worked, slowing them down and causing the experienced men to either laugh at the neophytes or sneer at their lack of accomplishment. The hands were a clue, too. Newbies were always checking on the progress of their calluses, blisters, splinters and rope burns. Old-timers did not bother. Their hands had been burned, scraped, and scarred but the lifelong sailors knew the work still had to be done, no matter the pain and discomfort of a few bruises.

Merlin came below deck when the storms tossed the ship and he had trouble holding on to the ropes. Stupid Bird refused to leave my shoulder, even during the worst storms. I put the parrot in its cage at night. He was too stupid to be left unattended and I did not want him getting out by accident. The captain hated the little beast.

"Hold on, Maddie," I said to the ship's cat twining herself around my leg. "Let me put Stupid Bird away and then I can sit down."

Maddie was good enough company. At least she did not try to hurt me whenever I saw her. With Stupid Bird in his cage, Maddie curled up in my lap, happy to ignore her duties. Gerry claimed what a great mouser she was but I never saw her chase a mouse or a rat. How did so many of the vile creatures get on the ship in the first place? They were on every deck, climbing the ropes even up to the top of the main topsail.

Passengers did their best to hide food from the vermin. Maddie had to kill a ship rat now and then because she was still alive. There was no food to spare for cat treats. The worst part about the rats was waking up to find one nibbling on my hair.

Merlin was a much better mouser than Maddie. The crew liked that. They were not happy to have 'bird boy' on the ship, but once Merlin started killing the mice that Maddie seemed to hide from, they stopped with the nastiest of the nasty looks.

It did not stop the shoving.

Since my bird boy duties did not keep me busy all day and being idle on the ship allowed the crew to shove, push and trip me, I made sure to work for the cook. He had a strange job. His duties included cooking for the captain out of one set of barrels, sacks, casks and crates. Since the crew worked in shifts, the cook baked for them but his main job was to distribute foodstuffs for the men to cook for themselves when they were off duty.

Once he decided I was not poisoning anyone, he assigned me a specific chore. I delivered the captain's meal to him once a day. At first, I thought this may have been a reward for helping him with his work. The crew did not dare trip, shove or push me while I was carrying the captain's meal. Of course, the walk back to the cook was rife with such pranks. Crewmembers were not creative people.

This new arrangement worked fine for weeks. As far as I could see, the captain had one job a day on the ship, to check on the navigation log. He rarely walked the ship other than his Sunday scripture readings and his Monday morning chore assignments. The rest of the time, he stayed in his cabin sleeping and drinking. A few times, when I delivered his meal, he was scribbling in a ledger.

I carried supper from the cook across the ship to the captain's quarters. It took a few harsh words to get Stupid Bird to perch outside the door. Then I knocked. The captain answered after my fifth knock.

"What?" he asked.

"Supper, sir."

"Enter."

The room smelled horrible. The captain had been drinking. There was an empty cask on the floor, rolling along with the ship's movement.

"Over here."

When I approached him with his tray, his body odor overpowered me. I could not wait to get out of there.

"Anyone suspect you are not a boy?"

He had never spoken to me during a meal delivery other than to give me permission to enter, place his food and to leave. Caught off guard, I did not know what to say.

"No, sir."

"The crew is not the sharpest on the seas, but we should get to the New World. Come closer. I have forgotten how nice it is to look upon a smooth skinned maiden."

Fear seized my body. How could I escape? Disobeying the captain's orders could result in any kind of punishment for insubordination he could dream. Lashings, keelhauling, he could hang me in a cage over the side of the ship and wait for me to starve, or simply hang me. There had to be another way out. I hoped for a wave to rock the ship, shifting our position and allowing me to escape but none came.

One other idea came to mind. It could still end in me being punished but at least I would have earned it.

I pretended to trip on the empty cask, falling forward and dumped the full tray on the captain. He jumped up when the hot coffee hit his skin through his clothes. His face turned three different shades of red. For a moment, I feared I had made the absolute wrong choice.

"Uh, oh! Sorry, sir. I am a clumsy oaf. A thousand apologizes."

"Get out!"

I wasted no time obeying that order. It was the last time I ever delivered a tray to the captain.

The next time I saw Captain Harris I was visiting Horace again. It was the end of the day and the captain was coming in to check the traverse board to see if the ship was on course and on time.

"Get that bird out of my face!" he yelled. "You have one job! Do it without getting in my way!"

I scampered to get Stupid Bird away from the captain. A few crewmembers were nearby and heard him yell at me. Anyone on the seas that day heard him yell.

"Hey, bird boy," one of them called. "Sounds like the captain isn't too happy with you."

"Maybe we should teach you a lesson," another said in a menacing tone.

Four of them moved toward me, hate in their eyes, joyful

expectation in their smirks. I looked in all directions. There was no escape. Two of the men were cracking their knuckles and one picked up a rope. They closed in on me.

Chapter Sixteen

My legs wobbled as I took a few fearful steps backward. I knew there was no way to outrun the men. The ship was too small.

Awk! Awk!

Merlin, who had been circling above us, flew toward the men. Inches above the deck, Merlin swung his body putting his talons first. The men jumped back to avoid contact with the razor sharp nails. I forced my wobbling legs to the stairs and looked back. Merlin grabbed the mouse he was after as it ran in front of the gang. Within seconds I was sitting on my hay, knees to my chest, panting. The crewmembers would not risk coming down where the passengers were to hit me.

Up on my shoulder, Stupid Bird mocked me.

Rah! Stupid Bird! Rah!

The Raven's creeks and groans had become a kind of music for me as I lay in my space next to the goats and sheep. I concentrated on those sounds to block out the ugly noises coming from the passenger side of the blanket. Men belittled their families, women yelled at children. Babies cried all day and night. Other people prayed, begging Providence to guide us across the ocean to the New World. Concentrating on the ship's noises was how I got to sleep that night and many other nights.

Ship life was regimented and structured but never predictable. The ocean and weather made sure of that. We could be in the middle of a scripture reading or a prayer and the crew would have to drop everything to secure the riggings and sails from a sudden storm or unforeseen rough waters. Captain Harris always seemed pleased, though, when the lessons were cut short. He read in his loud voice of authority but with no earnestness. I had trouble keeping up with some of the verses because I was used to them in other languages. In the glen, we did not use English when reading from the Bible.

Things on the ship got a little strange somewhere in the middle of the sea crossing.

The cook refused to bake until the sailors ate the biscuits he had already made which were rancid. Even the worms in them were dead. The crew was hungry and very angry. The only time anyone spoke was to relay orders or chant to keep the work moving. Captain Harris stayed in his cabin as much as possible. The cook had a separate food supply for the captain so he was not hungry and did not want to hear the complaints from his men.

One day while Stupid Bird and I were on our morning walk along the deck, Gerry snapped.

"You have to feed us!" he yelled at the cook. "We will die soon!"

"You have food," the cook replied. "No new food 'til the old is gone."

"Eatin' those biscuits 'll kill us, too!"

The cook shrugged. "No new food 'til the old is gone."

"Fine!" Gerry picked up one of the buckets that held the stone-like biscuits. He was about to dump it over the side of the ship.

"Don't do it," Ephram warned. "They hang you for wasting food."

"I ain't wasting food," Gerry said. "This ain't food. And don't tell me what to do!"

"I can tell you to do anything I want," Ephram said. "Charles's brother is first mate. He'll have you flogged just for talking back to me."

"For talking back to him, not you!" Gerry yelled. He had put down the bucket, which was good. Gerry was nice to me that first day and I did not want to see him get hurt. He was yelling in Ephram's face, which was bad. If Ephram was right, Gerry could be in a great deal of trouble.

"He doesn't like you anyway!" Ephram yelled back. "He thinks you ain't strong enough to do your share of work!"

"Is that so?"

"Aye, it is! And he's right, too!"

I do not know who touched whom first but soon the two men were shoving each other. A crowd had gathered and men were taking sides. Ephram tripped Gerry and the shoving turned into a wrestling match. The crewmembers were betting on the fight, no one was trying to stop it. Gerry got his arm around Ephram's neck but Ephram slammed his head back and blood poured out of Gerry's nose. He let go and Ephram punched him in the stomach. They wrestled some more, one gaining only to have the other counter and have control. Finally, a large man stepped in and pulled Gerry off Ephram. It was Pierre, Charles' brother and the first mate.

"What is going on here?" he asked.

"Gerry attacked me," Ephram lied.

"That ain't so. I want a trial. Plenty of people saw the whole thing."

There was a prickling feeling on the back of my neck. Something did not seem quite right about what was happening to Gerry. I wanted to say I had seen the whole thing but knew standing up for Gerry might hurt his case instead of help him because no one liked me. I waited to see what would happen next.

Pierre paused for a moment. "No need to bother the captain. Gerry, you'll get four lashings with the cat o' nine tails."

"What about Ephram?" Gerry asked. "Won't he be punished for fighting?"

"Five lashings. You want to question my authority again?"

The entire ship went silent. I could hear the water sloshing along the sides of the ship. Even the birds were quiet. It was eerie.

Pierre broke the silence by ordering Charles to get his cat o' nine tails. As we waited, the call went out for all hands to attend the lashing on the deck. I could not believe what was happening. Gerry had done nothing more wrong than Ephram had and neither deserved to be whipped. At home in the glen, wasting food was a serious offense, too, but Gerry had not thrown the biscuits over the side. Should there not be a hearing, at least?

By the time Charles arrived with the weapon, a huge crowd had gathered.

"Prepare yourself," Pierre ordered Gerry.

With blood still dripping from his nose, Gerry took off his shirt and grabbed the nearby mast.

"For trying to waste food, fighting on deck, and questioning my authority, Gerry Sullivan, you are sentenced to five lashings." Pierre raised the weapon in the air. Just as he started to whip it forward, someone took the handle out of his hand. Captain Harris.

At last! Sanity would prevail. Surely, the captain would not allow the lashing without a trial.

"What is this?" he asked in an even voice.

"Punishment for an offense, sir," Pierre replied.

"What offense?"

"He tried to waste food and then fought with the man who stopped him."

"And how much food was wasted in the incident?" Captain Harris's face twisted into a sneer. I got the impression he was not happy with Pierre.

"None, sir."

"For this small offense you intend to give how many lashings?"

"Five, sir."

Through all this, Gerry stood frozen, hands still above his head holding on to the mast. I held my breath, waiting for the captain to stop the lashing. Maybe he would even lash Pierre instead for abusing his authority.

The captain tapped the handle of the cat o' nine tails in his palm. Pierre looked nervous. Every member of the crew kept his eyes on the captain, including me. What would he do?

"Charles, get me a bucket of seawater." He smiled.

The crowd let out its collective breath. Men nudged each other in an excited way. Gerry stiffened. What did seawater have to do with anything? Charles fetched the bucket. Captain Harris dunked the tails into the seawater. The crowd cheered! Then he handed the weapon back to Pierre.

Whhiiip!

I flinched with every whip of the cat o' nine tails.

Whhiiip!

The whips cut into Gerry's skin leaving vicious bloody marks on his back.

Whhiiip!

Gerry tried not to scream but made garbled animal noises.

Whhiiip!

When the salty seawater hit the bloody gashes, it burned, intensifying the pain.

Whhiiip!

When the lashing was over, I turned aside so no one would see my tears. I had seen and even experienced punishments in the glen but they were always warranted. Gerry's lashing was just power gone awry. They were using punishment as entertainment. It was simply wrong.

Chapter Seventeen

My stomach felt like a hollowed out pumpkin sinking in on itself. As cheering from the men calmed down, Gerry limped off toward the forecastle. I wanted to tell him how sorry I was for how he had been treated and instruct him on how to treat the wounds but knew it would be of no help to him. I went back to my own bunk and cried.

The next day I tried to get my mind off Gerry by telling Stupid Bird one of my clan stories. He understood nothing, of course, but hearing them aloud helped me remember the tales. I had to make sure no one was around to hear me. Being able to tell the clan's history was one of the reasons my uncle and father sent me from the glen. I had to remember them well. To remember the songs, I tried to fit the words to the music the Raven made. At times, the creeks and groans fit the lyrics quite well.

One night, I fell asleep listening to the ship. I dreamt about sitting around the large clan fire, singing with my family, stealing glances at Gilbert and smiling. Then the flames turned green and purple. The rest of the clan disappeared and strange winged creatures flew toward me. I woke up to the sound of my own scream. No one heard me, though. There was too much commotion on the ship and I was not the only one screaming.

Awk!! Awk!! Merlin had flown down from the deck. He only did that when the ropes were unsafe because of rough seas.

The ship tilted to the side and I rolled under the blanket to the passengers' side. They were huddled together crying, screaming and praying. Water dripped through the ceiling. The ship continued to toss from side to side. We had been through rough seas before but this was brutal.

Light flashed through the seams in the wood and seconds later loud rolling sounds grumbled in the sky. A storm. A big one. Without knowing what I could do to help, I grabbed my cap and ran up the stairs.

I saw the sky first. It was the deepest black I had ever seen. The water was almost purple. Not a beautiful purple like the heather in springtime back home but ugly purple like a deep bruise.

Crewmembers hurried about in a kind of organized chaos. The noises were deafening. First mate Pierre was on one side of the ship and Harold the bosun was on the other. They joined in the work as they shouted orders to the men. Together the crew fought to control the rigging and the sails. Captain Harris stood in the middle yelling orders to everyone. They were using words I did not understand.

"Full swell on the larboard bow! Starboard ho!" one of the few men who had climbed the rigging yelled out. The job of these men, who held on with all their might, was to watch the ocean from a higher point than the deck and yell out what they saw. The captain, navigator, first mate and bosun used what they yelled to give orders to the crew.

"Larboard ho!" Pierre yelled. The men grabbed one set of ropes and started pulling the sails to send us in the opposite direction as the wave swell.

"Larboard bow! Starboard ho!"

"Larboard or Starboard bow?" Pierre yelled his question.

"Larboard bow!" the man in the rigging called. "The side we load from port on!"

"Larboard bow! Starboard ho!" Pierre ordered the correction and the men pulled the ropes again.

Critical moments were lost during the confusion. We sailed into the worst of the waves instead of away from them for several minutes. How could the words for left and right be so similar? Someone needed to change that.

Pierre yelled more words I did not understand, some because the turbulent storm drowned him out and some that I had not heard before. I realized I was the only one on deck not working. I ran toward one of the ropes. The ship tilted to one side and water covered the deck. My feet slid out from under me and I fell, banging my head against the deck. Lightning singed the sky in a pitchfork shape. There was a burning smell in the air.

I rubbed the back of my head and got up. This time I moved more carefully. Picking up slack in the rope, I pulled when the men yelled, "Heave!" and shifted my hands down the rope when they yelled "Ho!"

The wind took a violent change in direction and a huge wave tilted the ship. The Raven was almost on her side. Anything not tied down on the deck slid into the ocean. I had to hold onto the rope with all my strength, dangling in the air over the ship's deck. One man screamed as he slipped off the rigging and plunged into the ocean. I gulped hard to keep myself in control.

A few men put a rope sideways across the deck and half-slipped, half-climbed down, tying it off on the starboard railing. Moments passed before the waves returned the ship to a flatter but still dangerous pitch. I could put my feet on the deck again.

"Man up!" Harold yelled.

"Man up!" one of the men on the rope line with me dropped the rope and climbed up the same rigging that had just thrown another crewmember into the sea. The crew had to work together, even losing a few members, in order for the group to survive. Just like in the glen.

I pulled as hard as the others did, not knowing where the strength came from. No one knew I was a girl and now was not the time for them to find out. Blisters broke and bled on my hands while rope splinters bit into my palms. Muscles I did not know I had screamed for relief.

The noises got louder as the ocean roared an angry, taunting laughter.

My heart beat as fast as a hare's. It was the first time since I got to the ship that the ocean's movement made me queasy. My arm strength ran out and I slipped again. This time I kept sliding, feet first, toward the raging ocean. I grabbed at the sideways rope but my hands were too slick with seawater, sweat and blood, a stinging painful combination. Just as it occurred to me to aim my feet toward the railing, a wave hit the ship and knocked me into the purple brine.

Chapter Eighteen

Being swallowed by the ocean was a strange sensation. Bubbles swirled around me in eerie patterns, making it difficult to tell in which direction I was moving. Panic would have been the normal reaction, but it was not what came over me. Turmoil, uncertainty and disorientation tangled my mind. My lungs ached with the need for air. Surrounded by darkness, I tried to force my mind to focus, concentrate. Find a way to figure out which way to go.

Somewhere out the corner of my left eye, I saw a quick bright light. Flash, flash. Darkness. Flash, flash, flash. Lightning. That must be the way up to the top.

Kicking my legs and wriggling my shoulders in rhythm, I swam toward the lightning. I broke through the surface, choking, spitting, and gasping. Another lightning strike lit the sky and I saw the ship. I swam toward the Raven.

The ocean waves were ruthless, fighting my every motion, forcing water down my throat. My arms grew heavier with every stroke. I was close to the ship but so tired at the same time. It occurred to me to give up. Just stop swimming and let the cold ocean consume me. The thought of being safe with my mother, my friends and my ancestors was tempting. What was I struggling for anyway? What was waiting for me in the New World?

The wind blew foam in my face and I choked for breath. Something deep inside of me fought for life even though my brain was telling me to give up. Clan pride? Highland stubbornness? Perhaps I wanted to see what would happen next. I wanted to live.

A big wave swelled up from under me, lifting and carrying me toward the ship. The dead-tired feeling in my arms lightened and I was able to swim with the power of the wave beneath me.

Rigging on the ship started up by the sails and ended at the water. With the wave's help, I swam to the Raven and grabbed onto the web of ropes. The wave rolled under the ship causing it to tilt away from me at first and then back toward me. My back slammed into the ocean. I held on to the ropes and willed myself to stay out of the waves. The ship righted a bit and I started to climb up, trying to reach the deck. Another wave rocked the ship and my hands slipped. Desperate to stay out of the water this time, I grasped the ropes again.

"If at first you don't succeed, said the Bruce," I said aloud. "Try, try, and try again."

It was the ending of another story to remember, the legend of King Robert the Bruce and an unrelenting spider who refused to give up. I had to be that spider.

I climbed and climbed, slipped, grabbed and climbed some more. Finally, I reached the deck. When I threw my arm over the railing, a crewmember came over and pulled me to the safety of the ship. It was Gerry.

"Thought we lost ya," he said. He was gone before I could thank him, back on the rope.

I sat for a few minutes, catching my breath, feeling the cold in my body. Then I got up and took my spot on the line. There was still work to be done. My cap was near my spot on the rope line. It must come off when I fell. I put it back on. Some of the men nodded to me. I nodded back.

Soon after my return, the winds died down a bit. Lightning no longer left a smell and the thunder sounded further away each time. The storm was ending. It took the entire crew over an hour after the last flash of lightning to return the ship to some kind of normalcy. I helped where I could.

In the end, the captain gathered us together for prayers. He said a burial at sea prayer for the crewmember who was lost. I realized I did not know his name until Captain Harris committed him to the Lord's keeping. The crew muttered "Amen." Then he began the tempest prayer. It talked about waves lifting and carrying us as if to heaven. The prayer described what had happened to me when I got back to the Raven. Sadness and elation competed for space in my exhausted body. I had never felt a prayer so thoroughly. The session ended with another smattering of "Amen's" from the men.

"First watch!" Harold yelled.

Every crewmember who was not assigned to the first watch trudged to the forecastle. I wondered if they ate or slept first.

I was grateful to have survived the ocean. All that was in my mind on the way down to the tween deck was how glorious sleeping in my pile of dirty, dank, stinky hay was going to feel. I did what I always did when I needed to feel stronger. I reached up to feel my mother's stone.

It was not there. I ran my hand along my neck but did not feel the leather strap.

Gone? How could it be gone! That stone was not just the one thing I had left of my mother, my family but it was the only way to prove who I was, to show my aunt that I was her niece, her blood. Without that stone, my uncle would not pay my fare, I would be beholden to Captain Harris forever, destined to clean his wife's house or worse yet, be a boy on his ship. How could this have happened?

I turned around and went back up the stairs. Most likely, I had lost the necklace during my struggle in the ocean but I had to check every inch of the ship to be sure. The first place I looked was the rigging where I had pulled with the crew. Running my hands along every inch of rope took time. It was not there. I checked the railings, hoping to see the leather strap wrapped around the wood. Nothing. Next, I searched the forecastle, steerage and every storage area. There was no sign of my most prized possession. With tired, shaking legs, I climbed part way down the rigging to see if it had gotten caught in the web of ropes.

I did not see it anywhere. It was gone.

Chapter Nineteen

When I realized my mother's necklace was gone forever, all the things that I had lost in the last months, all my clans people, my home, my country, my place in society, my tartan blanket and now my mother's necklace, hit me harder than the waves. I could not breathe.

With nothing left to do but try to figure a way out of the contract I signed but could not read, exhaustion took over. I headed down to my dank, smelly hay with a heavy heart and dread in my stomach.

Stupid Bird was still in his cage. Merlin was also perch nearby, even though the seas were calmer. I collapsed into the hay, buried my face in my cap and cried. The worthless Maddie purred as she licked the salty tears from my face with her burlap tongue.

Awk! Awk!

"Quiet, Merlin," I said through choked tears.

Awk! Awk!

His call sound strange, muffled. I lifted my head out of my cap and looked up at Merlin. There, hanging in his beak was my leather strap, with mother's cairngorm dangling from it.

"Merlin!" I jumped up to my knees when I spoke. My heart and stomach jumped with me. Maddie brushed up against my legs. Could this be? Had Merlin saved us?

"Did it come off when the storm woke me? Has it been down here with you all this time?"

Merlin dropped the necklace in the hay next to me as an answer.

I picked it up, incredulous that I had it in my hand again. I draped it around my neck and tied the strap five times. This was my only chance at a life in the New World. I could never let it go again.

"Merlin, if I did not know that you would peck my eyes out, I would hug the feathers off you!"

I hugged Maddie instead. At least she was good for something.

That night was the one night on the Raven that I slept in deep, thorough peace.

That peace did not last. As we got closer to land, Captain Harris became more and more demanding. The men were even busier than usual. In addition to sailing the ship, the crew was shifting barrels, chests and crates around. Something about preparing for the customs check when we arrived in port. It seemed the captain wanted to hide the heavier and more expensive items to avoid paying high duties and taxes when the Raven off loaded.

The crew was still getting in cheap shots at me whenever they could. Gerry did not help anymore so at least I had won over one person. One evening, Stupid Bird and I were on the deck watching the sunset, my arms wrapped around my body. The sun warmed my skin but the wind carried cool air from the still cold waters. Two large shadows appeared around me. Soon I realized what they were.

"Pretty li'l scene, in't it Gavin?"

"Aye, a pretty li'l scene it is."

"It seems the bird boy is enjoying some free time. Takin' it all in."

"And why not? He has so much free time to fill."

Rah! Stupid Bird! Rah!

"Know wha' I been wonderin', Gavin. If we have a bird boy on board, why can't he keep the bird quiet?"

"Seems he's not a very good bird boy, eh?"

A wave rocked the ship and jostled some barrels that were stacked on the deck. It knocked me to the side as well. I steadied myself on the teetering barrels. I must have leaned too hard because the barrels fell and rolled toward the two men, tripping them up. As the men wrestled with the barrels, I ran in the opposite direction.

"You betta' run, you lousy twit!" one of the men yelled from the deck.

I ducked into steerage, glad to escape the beating. Horace never cared when I entered his domain, mainly because Stupid Bird had to stay outside.

From my hiding spot, I could hear Pierre screaming at Gavin and his pal to clean up the mess they had made before he ordered more lashings. It would have been fitting if he had. To be sure that the men were not waiting for me when I left, I waited for the watch change before returning to my bunk.

In many ways, I could not wait until we docked. I would be rid of the crew's constant badgering. They were nothing like the lads back home. The Hendersons and some others liked to tease but it was nothing compared to the taunts and physical pranks of the crewmembers. Again, I hoped Calum had made it home. Completing his task of getting me to Greenock would earn him some respect from the lads, but not as much as he hoped. I was also looking forward to real food, a clean bed, and wearing clothes made for a lass. Clean clothes made for a lass. I missed my skirts. Also, listening to constant English for weeks on end made my head throb with pain. At times, it was almost more than I could bear. I looked forward to telling Stupid Bird my stories because they were in my beloved mother tongue. Surely, my aunt would speak to me in Gaelic.

The best part of getting off the ship would be getting rid of Stupid Bird. That pirate had been clever to trick the captain into 'winning' that creature. I did not blame the captain for wanting the pirate to suffer the fate of living with the parrot again.

The closer we got to the New World the more nervous I became. What if the necklace was not enough to persuade my aunt that we were blood relation? What if she believed me but my uncle refused to pay my fare? Or could not pay? Would the captain be fair in negotiating a price? Was my uncle a fair man? Was he kind? I had to remind myself of their names, Justin and Orlie Cooper. I had heard their names so rarely in the glen that Calum and I were half way to Greenock before I could be sure I had the correct names. There were other fears as well. What if they did not live in Massachusetts Bay colony anymore? People moved all the time in the New World. Were they even alive?

That last thought kept me awake the last night on the ship. The seas were calm but my stomach flopped around. I lay in the now filthy hay, rubbing my mother's cairngorm between my fingers. If my aunt and uncle were dead or otherwise did not claim me, I told myself I could live with the captain's wife. Being a servant had its own kind of honor. The one thing I could not stand to think about was spending the rest of my life with Stupid Bird on my shoulder.

Chapter Twenty

Shaking, I arose from my hay bunk for the last time. At least, I hoped it was my last time. I could not think about the possibility that I would be trapped on that ship with Stupid Bird. Another thought came to me. What if the captain left the parrot with his wife and made me her house servant? Ugh. There was little I could do about it from the tween deck. I had to go up and face the day, whatever it brought.

Bringing the ship into port turned out to be a complicated undertaking. The crew had to maneuver the ship's sails, riggings and the Raven herself around other ships and their sails and riggings. I did what I could to help but with Stupid Bird on my shoulder, the crew did not appreciate me. Every ship had a cut out in the railing on the left side where the crew attached the gangplank. All the ships pulled in with the port on that side. Why not just call it the port side instead of larboard and avoid all the confusion?

After securing the gangplank, the men had to unload all the goods for customs inspection. The passengers offloaded themselves and dealt with the customs agents alone. I was glad that I had no possessions, except my necklace, which was well hidden from view under my shirt. My hand slipped to it every chance I had to make sure it was still there.

Paying duties and taxes to the customs agents was an important part of the captain's job. Fees brought money for the government and the community but the captain did not want to pay more than necessary so that his risky ocean journey netted him a profit as well. Customs agents were always looking for anything extra they could tax to increase the fees and the captains were always hiding the real value of things to lower the fees. The give and take of Captain Harris and the customs agent went on for a while, each accusing the other of cheating, in the most courteous terms and tones, of course. One must be civil, after all.

Watching Captain Harris negotiate his fee made me realize that he was a different person on land than at sea. On the ship, he wanted everything done with the least fuss. Often staying in his cabin to avoid confrontation, letting Pierre, Harold and Horace deal with unpleasantries until his presence was needed. On land, he thrived on making a deal, diving into complicated situations with glee and talking in circles until the other person was so dizzy he could not remember what his original stand was. It was almost enough to make me smile. Almost.

While I watched and listened to the captain, I waited for my chance to ask about finding my aunt and uncle. We had sailed into a small town north of Boston. All I knew about my uncle was his name and that he had lived in a small port city in the Massachusetts Bay colony. I hoped it would be enough to find him.

"Thank you, sir and have a splendid day," Captain Harris said as the tax assessor walked away, studying his ledger and scratching his head. The captain was smiling so I decided it was okay to approach him.

"Excuse me, captain, sir," I said.

"Uh, you," he said as he saw me. "I see you survived the trip. To be honest, I was not sure you would. Well, I guess it's time to find your father."

"Uncle, sir."

"Ah, yes. Your uncle. His name?"

"Mister Justin Cooper, sir."

"Fine. You have until the ship is unloaded to find someone who knows your uncle."

What? How was I supposed to do that?

"Can you offer any assistance, sir?"

"I am a busy man. No time to go traipsing around the docks. And take that bird with you. If your uncle can not be found, you will be carrying that parrot to my house yourself."

No time to help me? He did not believe I had any chance of finding my uncle! I knew he was not an honorable man. He thinks I will be his housemaid for years. If I did not find my uncle, I would be.

How could the captain afford to let me wander off by myself? Stupid Bird was still on my shoulder, I had no money and no idea where I was. He knew I could not go far. I had to find someone who knew Justin Cooper and I needed to find that person now. I headed over to the next dock and started my search.

The port was crowded with all kinds of people. Sailors, customs agents, American Indians, slaves, tradesman, merchants and other townspeople. The barrels, crates, boxes and trunks that were stacked all around made it even more difficult to see where I was going. Time and time again, I asked each person if he knew Justin Cooper. The people I came across did not seem happy to stop their work to answer my question. It was a good thing I was still dressed in my servant boy clothes or none of them would have talked to me at all. Of course, Stupid Bird refused to be quiet.

I asked one man who was unloading crates branded with a skull and cross bones.

"Aye, I know Justin Cooper."

My heartbeat quickened. He was alive! He lived nearby!

"What business do you have with him?" the man asked.

"I have news of his family." Sticking to the truth would help the most. "Do you know where he is now?"

"No. This time of day, he could be anywhere."

I sped off with a renewed spirit of possibility.

A few other people said they knew my uncle but offered no further help. My hope dimmed and I imagined myself scrubbing chamber pots with a parrot on my shoulder, when a man approached me. He was tall with deep blue eyes and brown hair. He wore no beard or mustache but did have a large brimmed hat.

"Are you the lad looking for Justin Cooper?" he asked.

"Aye, sir," I said. "Do you know him?"

"What business do you have with him?"

"I…I…" what could I say to make him help me find my uncle? "I have news from Scotland. Glencoe, sir."

"Glencoe?" he asked. He grabbed me by my shoulders, lifting me so only the tips of my toes still touched the ground. Instead of flying off, Stupid Bird grabbed harder onto my shoulder. "You know of Orlie's family? What? Tell me what you know. All we have heard is that the MacIain was slain. My wife is sick with worry about her family!"

He knew about MacIain?

"Your wife is Orlie?" I asked. "Orlie Cooper?"

"Yes, yes. Tell me what you know about her family." He shook me, hard enough to snap my head back. My cap fell to the ground.

"You are Justin Cooper?"

"Aye, yes. Tell me lad. What do you know of the massacre at Glencoe?"

Chapter Twenty-One

My body buzzed with competing emotions. Confusion, fear, relief, sadness, hope. This man said he was Justin Cooper. Married to Orlie Cooper. Could it be? He knew the MacIain and Glencoe. He called it a massacre. He could be my uncle. Had I found him? The man I hoped could rescue me from the captain and Stupid Bird. I had to be sure before I told him who I was.

"I have sad news, sir," I told him. He squeezed my arms so tight I thought they would burst.

"Margaret is dead." It pained me to say it.

Justin Cooper dropped his grip on my arms and looked up at the sky. Stupid Bird's grip loosened, too.

"Dead. Killed by the Redcoats?"

"After, sir. When we were hiding in the woods. She froze or starved."

He lowered his eyes to mine. For a moment, I feared he might grab hold of me again. "Alasdair. What of him?"

"He survived. The last I saw he was on his way to Edinburgh. That was months ago, now, sir."

"The children? Did any of them survive?"

"Aye, sir. The one child still in their home survived."

"Baby Dory?"

I took a deep breath before my next sentence.

"I am not a baby anymore, sir," I said. It did not take him long to catch my meaning.

"Dory?" he asked. "I thought you were a lass."

"Aye, I am, sir. The captain made me dress like a lad so I could blend in with the crew."

"He made you work on a crew?" Alarm and anger filled his voice.

"No, sir. I took care of his parrot and my buzzard, Merlin. They called me the bird boy."

"Are you hurt? Were you injured in any way?" He seemed sincere when he asked about my injuries. I judged Justin Cooper to be an honorable man. Hope overrode the other emotions swirling in my body.

"I am fine, sir. But the captain will be looking for me soon."

"Did you run away?"

"No, he gave me until the ship was unloaded to find you." I looked down for a moment. It was a shameful thing to ask for money. Even from family. "I told him you would pay my fare when we arrived."

"I see," he said. "What was the plan if you could not find me?"

"I was to be his wife's servant until I earned my fare. I had no choice, sir. My uncle, my other uncle, sent me here. He is the new chief and he wanted a MacDonald of Glencoe to survive in case the Redcoats came back to finish the job of killing us all. He and my father decided to send me after my mother died. They gave me this to prove who I was."

I pulled my necklace out of my shirt. He looked at it.

"A cairngorm, I see." My knees buckled with relief for a moment. "It does look like Orlie's."

He paused for a moment studying the necklace.

"Where is this sea captain?" he asked.

"Captain Harris sails the Raven," I told him. "Fifth ship down."

"The bird stays with him?"

Rah! Stupid Bird! Rah!

"The parrot does," I said. "Merlin belongs to me. He is no trouble, I promise. He even finds his own food."

"Where is this Merlin?"

"I am not sure," I confessed. "He shows up when he needs to."

"It seems you do not have a choice about whether or not he comes with you."

I did not answer. He had not said he would pay the captain, yet. I could not risk angering him.

"Let us go see this captain of yours."

I walked with Justin Cooper, the man who may be my uncle. Many people paused to tip their hats to him and he returned the gesture. At one point, he stopped a man in a wagon and spoke to him in hushed tones. The man nodded, slapped the reins on the horse's backside and took off. We walked on in silence.

Justin Cooper had me wait at a distance when he approached Captain Harris. I have no idea what they said but they spoke for a very long time. The captain did not look happy. He looked surprised, then angry. As I waited, exhaustion hit me. My feet and my head ached. Even as these two men discussed my future, I longed to lie down and sleep.

As I tried to catch bits of their conversation, I noticed the dock-workers began to leave, a wagonload at a time. The few men left on the docks guarded groups of crates, chests, barrels and trunks. There must have been a big event happening in town. I watched as the docks became more than half-empty.

One lone wagon came toward the docks. It carried the man my uncle had spoken with earlier and a woman. She sat tall on the bench, her hands in her lap. From a distance, I could see her bright white collar, cuffs, bonnet and apron. She kept her head square on her shoulders, facing in front of her.

The man stopped the wagon in front of the Raven. The captain and my uncle continued their conversation and neither person in the wagon moved. How much longer would I need to wait before I knew my fate? Finally, Captain Harris looked over at me.

"Come, here," he called.

Rah! Stupid Bird! Rah!

I walked to the group. At the same time, Justin Cooper helped the woman, whom I assumed was Orlie Cooper, down from the wagon.

We stood together looking at each other.

Aunt Orlie was beautiful. Dark hair pulled in a tight bun tucked under her crisp white bonnet. She looked so much like Mother I wanted to fall into her arms, weep and never let her go. Then I remembered where mother was, buried alone in the cold, covered with rocks. The warm feeling of love that had rushed through my body cooled just as quick.

"Take off your hat," the captain said.

I followed his instruction. I had not seen clean warm water in months while trekking through the wilderness and pretending to be a boy on a cross-ocean voyage. I had to look frightening.

"She has a cairngorm," my uncle said. "And claimed to be from Glencoe. Not many people would have that combination. Take out your necklace, lass."

"Stop," Orlie Cooper said. "I do not want to see it."

What? How could she say that? How could she disown me without seeing my proof? Disappointment crushed the air out of my lungs. Tears welled in my eyes. Then she spoke again.

"This is my sister's child."

What? How could she know without seeing my cairngorm?

"You are sure?" my uncle asked.

Rah! Stupid Bird! Rah!

"We must get her home. She needs to change out of those shameful clothes and have a good scrubbing."

The purest joy filled my heart. My mother's sister claimed me to be her blood relation. I was too afraid to smile, though. The terms of the contract had yet to be settled.

"We have an agreement, then?" the captain asked.

"You are entitled to your fare, sir," my uncle said.

I was almost free. Almost. I dared not move, standing still waiting for orders.

Captain Harris sent me onto the Raven to get Stupid Bird's cage while he and my uncle finished their business. I replaced my cap and ran up the gangplank. The crew was continuing to offload the cargo and therefore had no time to harass me with punches or trips as I made my way through the ship. When I reached up for the cage, something touched my leg. Even with all my time at sea, I still hated the feeling of rats and mice brushing against me. Then I heard Maddie meow. I bent over and picked her up.

"Goodbye little Maddie," I said. "I hope you get to stay on land for a while."

Spooked by the noise of a barrel rolling overhead, Maddie scratched the back of my hand and escaped out of my arms. A fitting farewell.

I rubbed the scratch mark then grabbed the cage. It took a few tries to convince Stupid Bird to get into the wooden enclosure but eventually he did.

Rah! Stupid Bird! Rah!

"Well, Stupid Bird," I said. "You are getting your old friend back, Captain Harris."

Silence. I wondered if Stupid Bird had understood me.

I climbed the stairs and walked on the Raven's deck for the last time. Worry and excitement jumbled in my stomach. Justin and Orlie Cooper seemed to be good and honest people. I hoped that turned out to be true. They did not seem to like me, though. Of course, they were in the middle of a business transaction and my arrival had been a complete surprise. Still, it would have been nice if Aunt Orlie had hugged me. She had called my clothes shameful, which they were and said I needed a good scrubbing, which I did. So what was bothering me about them?

I came down the gangplank at a much slower pace than I had run up it. I passed Gerry on the way. He sort of half nodded. I smiled. Back at the wagon, Captain Harris did not smile when I handed the parrot back to him.

I did not look at my aunt and uncle. It was easier to defer to the captain.

"Your uncle has paid your fare and this man has served as witness," Captain Harris said, nodding to the man who was driving the wagon. "You are released from our contract."

Relief made my knees weak. No more pranks from the crewmembers. No more Stupid Bird. No more captain.

"Thank you, sir," I said. Once the captain had no power over me, I had to look at my new family. I raised my eyes to meet Aunt Orlie's.

"Get in the back of the wagon, Dory," she said. She pronounced my name the English way. Not the way mother had.

"Aye, ma'am."

As quick as possible, I walked to the back of the wagon and climbed in. My uncle helped Aunt Orlie climb onto the bench seat before hoisting himself up next to her. With all three adults crammed onto the bench, the driver turned the wagon around and headed away from the water.

My stomach dropped. I was happy to be free from life on the Raven, but what would happen next?

"Take off that hat and undo what's left of your braid," Aunt Orlie said over her shoulder. "Do you know how to wear your hair in a bun?"

I was already trying to unsnag my tangled hair when I answered. "Aye, ma'am."

"Fine. There are clothes at our home that will fit you with little sewing. Do you sew?"

"Aye, ma'am. A bit."

"We will work on that, too."

"Too, ma'am?" I asked.

"Things are different here than you are used to, child. There will be many things for you to learn."

Aunt Orlie's manner was stiff and she seemed to be speaking in some kind of code. Perhaps she did not want the wagon driver to know the details of family business. At home, everyone in the glen knew your business but we did not share with outsiders.

The town was small with well-built homes and shops. Smoke curled out of every chimney even though the temperature was quite warm. Very warm. I wondered how long it had been since I left home.

"Pardon me, ma'am," I ventured. "What is the date?"

"The tenth of June," she answered.

Four months. I had been on the run for four months.

No one spoke for a while. We bumped along the well-worn road.

People were gathering around a tree on a nearby hill. This must be where the workers from the docks had gone. A big stir parted the crowd and a wagon pulled by a pair of oxen appeared in view. A woman stood in the back, holding on to a high wooden bar.

"Beg, pardon, ma'am," I said. "What are they doing?"

"Hanging a witch," Uncle said.

"A witch? I do not know that English word." I asked. "What is a witch?"

"Bana-bhuidseach," Aunt Orlie whispered. It was the first word of my beautiful Gaelic that I had heard in months. It meant sorceress, a person who used evil powers obtained through a deal with the devil. The kind of wicked person Calum feared.

"Aye, ma'am." It was all I could think to say.

"Everyone in Salem has gone mad," Uncle said to no one in particular. I had fled my home while being a hunted fugitive, survived nasty crewmates and a near-drowning at sea all to get here, a place where people were dealing with the devil.

What had I done?

Chapter Twenty-Two

As the wagon continued to bump out of town, I wondered about how Uncle had known about what happened in the glen. It had taken Calum and me months to get to Greenock and there would have been ships leaving Scotland almost every day. The news must have crossed the ocean with some of those people. I decided not to ask any more questions for a while. Not even about how everyone in town had gone mad.

Uncle Justin and Aunt Orlie lived near town but on a small farm with pigs. Aunt Orlie and I climbed down from the wagon. Uncle and the wagon driver drove away.

"I did not want to correct you in front of John," Aunt Orlie said, "but in Salem, children only speak in the presence of adults when adults speak to them. It is different here but you will learn."

Ashamed of my behavior, I lowered my head. My instinct was to apologize but then was unsure if Aunt Orlie had given me permission to speak.

"We can be more relaxed at home but please be mindful that your Uncle is from the English, not the Scottish Highland, tradition."

"Aye, ma'am." For some reason, tears threatened to drip from my eyes. I fought them.

Aunt Orlie nodded and got to work. She told me to wait for her in the barn and went into the house. There were many tools and a large bench in the barn. I noticed a large wooden tub in the corner. When Aunt Orlie returned, she had a thick wooden plank with bristles on one-half of one side. It was a hairbrush but in the glen some mother's used hairbrushes to discipline their children. I winced when I saw it. Would Aunt Orlie use it to help me remember not to speak before spoken to in public?

"It is for your hair, child, not your backside," she said as if she had read my mind. "Brush out your hair while I heat some water. It will wash out better after a good brushing. First drag the tub closer to the door."

Relieved that I would not be beaten, I did as Aunt Orlie asked. I tipped the tub on its side and rolled it toward the door then went to work brushing my hair. Dirt and leaves as well as clumps of hair fell to the ground as I tugged the brush through. Aunt Orlie carried pots of hot water from the house and I helped her empty them into the tub. Once it was two-thirds full, she left me alone. The last time I had bathed was before the snow fell at home. Seeing the clean water turn a dirty grey was upsetting. Some of that dirt was from my homeland. I was washing Scotland off my skin and out of my hair. My reformed heart ached for the people I would not see again.

To distract my mind and keep myself from crying, I tried to think of the last time I had been alone. Not on the ship, that was for sure, especially if you counted Stupid Bird, which I did. Calum had been with me every second since we left the camp in the forest until we reached Greenock. Of course, I had felt alone the whole time. How could I not? My family and best friend were dead, gone from this earth forever.

It occurred to me that I had not seen Merlin since we left the Raven. I hoped he had followed us. I would have to trust that Gilbert had been right and Merlin would find me when he wanted. As I washed and thought, flying insects of various sizes gathered around the muddy water. They buzzed by my ears and destroyed the few solitary moments I had. As soon as I finished rinsing my hair the last time, I stepped out and dried off with a sheet that Aunt Orlie had left for me.

"Are you alright child?" She was standing in front of the open barn door. I wrapped the cloth around my body.

"Aye, ma'am," I said.

Sunlight streamed in through the open door. Aunt Orlie ran her fingers across the folded clothes in her hands.

"Your hair has red in it," she said.

"Aye, ma'am." Father always told me what a blessing it was that my hair shone red in the sun.

"Mine did, too, in my youth. The same with my daughter Margaret. But only when the light hit it, like yours."

I stayed quiet and still, wrapped in the sheet, water dripping off my nose.

"How much do you know about my leaving the glen?" she asked.

"Not much, ma'am."

"Justin, your uncle, came to Glencoe while he was traveling through the Highlands on his way to Edinburgh. He was so kind and so handsome that I fell in love straight away. Mother, Father and your mother begged me to stay but my young heart was foolish and anxious to be with Justin. He is a good man and we have had a good life here." She touched her hand to her collar and pulled out a leather strap with a gem dangling at the end. It was her cairngorm. It looked identical to Mother's, which was now mine. "That was when our father gave us the necklaces, so we could always know our family. I had not realized how much I missed Scotland until you came."

I stayed still, allowing flies to land on my head. Aunt Orlie continued.

"Salem is a small place. Everyone knows everything about everyone. Much like in the glen. But here, there is a separation. People who live near the docks are merchants, traders who work for their own gain. People in the village are more of a community but still not as much as we MacDonalds. The divide between town and village is getting worse with these witch accusations and Reverend Parris driving the fury. Dreadful business. I pray this will pass soon and our leaders will return to sanity before another life is lost."

The first life, I guessed, being the witch they had hung that day. It was not unusual for reverends to be involved with wicked things. It was one of their jobs, to keep the righteous from straying to the devil. There was, however, something in how Aunt Orlie spoke that frightened me. She did not sound as if she trusted this Reverend Parris. It appeared life in Salem would be difficult. I would have to do my best to make it work and pray every day that my father would send for me.

My stomach made an embarrassing gurgling sound.

"Here I am going on about town gossip when you have not seen proper food in months. Are you hungry, child?"

"Aye, ma'am."

She smiled. "There may be some cornbread and honey mead left over from the morning meal."

"Aye, ma'am." I had never heard of cornbread but would try it. Anything but oatmeal.

"My Margaret wore these clothes when she was your age," Aunt Orlie said as she put them on the small bench next to the door. "They should work well enough for a few days while we make something that fits you better."

I waited a few heartbeats before I asked my next question.

"I can stay, ma'am?"

Aunt Orlie looked at me. "Child, you are my blood. Not only are you our responsibility, you will come to be an important part of this family."

Did being a part of their family mean I would no longer be a part of mine? Did I have any family left in the glen? We looked at each other in silence again. I would become a part of their family if my father did not send for me. I intended to go back to Scotland as soon as it was safe. Then Aunt Orlie left me alone to change and think about what she said.

Margaret's dress should have touched the ground but ended somewhere above my ankles, instead. In the summer months in Glencoe, I would not have worn stockings or shoes but Aunt Orlie had included some with the other clothes. I pulled on the scratchy stockings and stepped into the little leather shoes. My toes would not fit into the small space and my heels hung over the other end. I took them off and slipped back into my boots. Even with a few wee holes in the bottoms and a rip or two in the tops, the boots fit better than the tiny shoes. I tied my damp hair up in a bun and covered it with the bright white bonnet. Then I headed to the house.

The front door was open but I waited for Aunt Orlie to see me. Acting timid did not come natural to me. It made me think of Calum, too. I wondered if I would ever know what became of him. I glanced inside as much as I dared. It was neat, clean and in perfect order, as I expected. Sunlight streamed in from the open door and the small windows of thin paper. Shutters stood on the outside of the house to protect the windows from bad weather. A fire burned in the fireplace.

"Come in, child," she said. "This is your home now."

The tears I had avoided in the barn sprang to my eyes. This was my home, not my glen in Scotland. I shook my head as if to shake the thought out of my mind. My parents wanted this for me. The chief wanted this for the clan. It had taken a minor miracle to find my uncle in the time the captain had given me. Perhaps someone or something else wanted this as well. Until I heard otherwise from my father, this was my home. I stepped inside.

The wooden floors were a surprise. In Glencoe, we had dirt floors. All around the room stood pieces of wooden furniture, a large bed tucked at one end, a long table, two benches and a stool closer to the fireplace. One chair sat at the end of the table. Stairs built near the table climbed to the attic. The stone fireplace took up most of one wall. It reminded me of Scotland where all the bothies were made of stone. Planks of wood made the roof in Salem, not the thatch that we used in the glen.

"Here you are, child." Aunt Orlie put a wooden trencher on the table with a mug. I knew that I should not expect such treatment on any other day. As the daughter, I did the serving at our house. In Glencoe, at my old house, that is.

"Thank you, ma'am," I said. The food smelled wonderful. I dug in. The bread tasted sweet and delicious. A few minutes into my meal, Aunt Orlie handed me a cloth napkin. I realized I was bent over my plate, shoveling food in my mouth like an animal. Apparently, I had been at sea too long. Embarrassed by my boorish behavior, I took the napkin, sat back and ate like the granddaughter of a clan chief that I was.

Aunt Orlie busied herself with folding linens.

"How many languages do you know?" she asked when I paused to breathe between bites.

"Five, ma'am," I answered with pride. "Gaelic, English, Scots, French and Latin."

"Can you read or write any of them?"

"No, ma'am." My pride diminished.

"That is fine," she said. "We can teach you to read and write English. You know your scripture lessons?"

"Well enough to satisfy Father, ma'am."

"And Urnaigh an Tighearna. Do you know that?"

"Aye, ma'am."

"In English?" she asked. "It is called the Lord's Prayer."

"Only in Gaelic, ma'am. And French." Seeing that this disappointed her I added. "I am sure I can learn it in English."

"You will have to," she said. "It is one of the tests."

"Tests, ma'am?"

"Aye. The ministers seem to think that witches cannot recite the Lord's Prayer without mistakes. It is part of the examination for suspected witches."

With my stomach satisfied for the first time since I could remember and my body in clean clothes, I had begun to feel stronger and my headache to fade. A trickle of fear wormed its way into my full stomach. This talk of witches disturbed me. Aunt Orlie spoke as if I would have to undergo an examination for suspected witches. If that were true, then Uncle was right. Everyone in Salem had gone mad. I decided to brave another question.

"Will you tell me more of these witches, ma'am?" I ventured.

"It is silliness gone awry. 'Witches' is the word they use here for anyone they believe is under control of the devil. Their main crime seems to be making young girls cry. It started months ago when a few girls became ill and the doctor proclaimed there was nothing to be done. The minister sat with them and declared them bewitched. Through prayer and fasting, they healed. Then Reverend Parris claimed his slave woman from Barbados, Tituba, confessed to bewitching the girls, one of whom was his own daughter. He claims the slave woman named others who were with her when she signed the devil's book. Soon, there were suspected witches everywhere. Not just in Salem but other towns, too, Andover, Beverly and Boston."

I nodded. Under the table, my hands twisted and untwisted the napkin.

"None of that is important right now. You must get used to your new home and routine as soon as possible. Justin will expect you to perform the same chores our Margaret did and I will teach you to read and write as you do them. You will have some freedoms on the farm but we must be careful. Anything can put you under suspicion. Do not speak anything but English when anyone else can hear you. Even your uncle."

"Would he suspect me a witch, ma'am?" I asked, alarmed.

"No, child. He would suspect it a more difficult task to protect you."

Squeals and snorts from the pigs arose to a new pitch. They sounded frightened. Uncle burst through the door and yelled.

"Child, come quickly! I believe I have found your buzzard!"

Chapter Twenty-Three

Merlin! Once again, my old friend found me when he wanted. When I arrived on the Raven, Captain Harris had said I liked to make an entrance. In truth, it was Merlin. I shook my head at him but said nothing. It would have wasted breath to scold him.

Merlin sat in a tree near the pig enclosure, resting on his left leg, unrepentant and relaxing in the mid-day heat.

"You have a bird?" Aunt Orlie asked. She looked fearful.

"He is quite tame, ma'am," I assured her. "He can hunt for himself. Mice and other small animals. In Glencoe, I had a leather glove with ties and I could call him to rest on my wrist. He has been free for so long now, I think it would be cruel to cage him again."

"You are right, child," Uncle said. "He needs no cage or leather ties. He found you when he wanted to, did he not?"

"But, Justin. What if someone sees her? They could claim he is a familiar."

"I know, Orlie," he said. He turned to me and made sure to look me in the eyes. "Child, you cannot be seen recognizing the bird. By anyone. Ever. Do you understand?"

"Aye, sir," I said. I understood the instruction but not why it he gave it. I hoped Merlin would understand the new rules.

"It is of the upmost importance, Dory," Aunt Orlie said, the fear still in her eyes. "No one can know that this bird responds to your orders."

"He does that when he feels like it."

"It is believed that the devil gives witches wild birds," Uncle said. "If anyone sees you conversing with a bird or one responding to you, they may accuse you of being a witch. If that happens, we cannot save you. You will be at the mercy of the courts, courts we do not trust right now. Do you understand?"

"Aye, sir." This was a frightening conversation. I thought about Gilbert and how it would hurt him to think that his heroic act of saving Merlin could cause me harm. I hoped Merlin would understand. My head began to throb again.

Uncle looked at me and gave a small smile.

"Margaret's clothes are a bit small for you," he said. "The two of you will fix that soon enough. There never seems to be enough time to keep up with the linens."

"Aye, sir." I was grateful for the change in topics. Thinking about chores was much easier than thinking about witches. Aunt Orlie was right. Uncle was a good kind man. I would be careful not to make him cross.

The pigs were getting used to seeing Merlin in the tree so Uncle went back to his own chores and Aunt Orlie and I returned to the house. She set me to baking more cornbread for the evening meal, telling me what to do and then leaving me to do it. As we cooked, she taught me the English words to the Lord's Prayer. We recited them over and over and over again. It sunk in how important it was to learn the proper wording and be able to recite it. Somehow, that made it harder to remember. My constant cough made it more difficult to recite the words smoothly.

With supper cooking, we set about making my new clothes. Still working on the prayer, of course. In the corner next to the spinning wheel there was a large basket filled with yarn that had been spun from flax. Aunt Orlie took out a hand held loom and threaded the yarn onto it. It was a bit different from the looms in the glen, but I picked up how it worked soon enough. Making cloth made me relax. It was simple. The yarn went on the loom, I worked it through the wooden frame and soon there would be cloth.

"No, Dory," Aunt Orlie said, her voice tinted more with annoyance than fear. "Bread, not pain. You're mixing it up with French again."

"Apologies, ma'am. I am awful tired."

"Of course, child. You will sleep well tonight, right after supper. But now you have to think, remember the words in English."

I was tired of English. I longed to hear my Gaelic. Would Aunt Orlie never speak to me in our beautiful language? Except for that one nasty word that meant a person in league with the devil. I was doomed to this English the rest of my days? Sighing to myself, I focused once again on the prayer.

I started again, faltering a few times, using a Gaelic word here and a French word there. Aunt Orlie continued to correct me and have me start from the beginning. It was tiring and made me weave much slower.

At the sound of a wagon outside, we both fell silent. There was a knock at the door.

Aunt Orlie put her finger to her lips, telling me to be quiet. Then she opened the door.

"Afternoon, Orlie," the man at the door said. "Is Justin home?"

"Good afternoon, Nicholas. I believe Justin is chopping wood with John."

"Were you at the hanging today?"

"No, we had business at the pier."

"It was a terrible sight. That witch Bridget Bishop swore to be innocent with her last breath. Even with the rope around her neck! They found poppets in her basement! Can you imagine?"

"I do not like this constant witch talk."

"No one likes it. However, it must be done if we hope to escape the powers of the devil."

Aunt Orlie did not answer because the man, Nicholas, caught sight of me. I was sitting on a stool, threading the loom and keeping an eye on the meal. I kept my head down but my eyes up, hoping the brim of my bonnet would hide them.

"Dory, come here." Aunt Orlie must have realized that he saw me. I got up and put my loom down on the stool. I kept my head down and walked to the door.

"Nicholas, this is my niece. She arrived today and will be living with us."

"Bless us. A new girl in your home. Martha will be pleased to hear of it. Let me see your eyes, child." I looked up into the man's face. His teeth were grey and dirt smudged his nose and cheeks. "She seems a good sort. Blessings to you, Orlie."

"Thank you, Nicholas."

"I will be sure to tell Martha of this joyous news at supper this eventime."

From all the talk of witches, I had half expected this stranger to haul me away to jail. I was relieved when he left.

At least he did not seem to think I was a witch. Perhaps minding my manners and staying out of trouble would be enough to keep me from having to say this prayer in English as a test. I was not sure I would pass.

After the door was shut and the man was gone Aunt Orlie stood still for a moment, like a fly surprised by an early winter frost. I waited, unsure what to do. Finally, she spoke.

"We must be careful. I would like as few people as possible to know that you came from the Scottish Highlands. We shall say you are from Scotland if someone asks, that should be good enough."

A flash of anger flared in my belly over the apparent insult.

"Do people here not like the Highlands, ma'am?"

"People do not trust what they do not know. They believe other people's mad tales of Highland savages instead of using the common sense the Lord granted them. It is better this way, child."

Hiding that I was from the Highlands, not speaking Gaelic, ignoring Merlin. I had to deny who I was in order to avoid being accused of witchcraft. I was not sure I would survive in Salem.

Chapter Twenty-Four

At the evening meal, I struggled to keep my heavy eyelids from falling. As uncle read the evening scriptures, my mind was too exhausted to make sense of the English words. The rhythm of his low, calm voice sounded like a lullaby. Only my need to cough kept me awake at the table.

When the scriptures were over Aunt Orlie gave me instructions.

"Your uncle tightened the bed upstairs and I put out fresh linens. We get up with the sun, but tomorrow you may sleep in. It would serve no purpose to make you perform your chores poorly because you are tired and ill. You need rest. I will not wake you."

I knew that I should say something, tell my aunt and uncle how much I appreciated them paying my fare and taking me into their home. But I was also hoping for a letter from my father, calling me back to Scotland. So many ideas swam in my head and I was too tired to sort through them all. Instead, I curtsied, as was the English custom, and trudged up the stairs, pulled off my bonnet, boots, apron, shirt and skirt. I put on the nightdress Aunt Orlie had left out for me. Then I fell into the bed and slept.

The sun was high in the sky when my stomach woke me and I opened my eyes. I could hear the pigs outside, squealing and oinking as Uncle did his chores. Aunt Orlie's shoes scraped across the wooden floor as she completed her indoor tasks.

Listening to the sounds of a home at work made me think of my old life in Scotland before the attack. In some ways, it was comforting to be in a normal home again but the memories of my parents, friends and clansmen made my heart sad and my head hurt.

I wanted to snuggle down and enjoy the dry, warm bed. The first one I had known in months. Nevertheless, staying abed any longer was not an option. Aunt Orlie had already given me extra time to sleep, it was time to get up and start on the day's chores. Changing out of my too-short nightclothes and into my too-short day clothes, loneliness and fear swelled up in my throat. My heart ached for my family and friends. These feelings always took me by surprise when they arose. I thought about them all the time but the loneliness hit when I was not expecting it. I swallowed hard and went down the stairs to my new life.

During my first few days with Aunt Orlie and Uncle, we settled into new routines. They had to get used to having another child in the house and I had to get used to everything while missing all the people I had lost. In the glen, as long as we obeyed our elders and otherwise stayed out of sight, we could do pretty much anything we wanted. In Salem, it was work all the time and then study the Bible.

I had to use English all the time. Along with reciting the Lord's Prayer, which I had to do before sitting down to each meal, Aunt Orlie began to teach me how to read and write English using our morning and evening scripture lessons.

"Many men and women learn to read and write in Salem. It is important to be able to do business and understand a document you are asked to sign."

Was she talking about the contract I signed with the captain back in Greenock? I wanted to explain how I had tried to protect myself even though I could not read the words. Would Aunt Orlie consider that talking back? I kept quiet.

The food took some getting used to as well. My new favorite was cornbread, which I had with honey mead to break my fast in the morning. I missed my mother's stew, though. My chores were similar to the ones from my old life. Working hard inside with Aunt Orlie meant cooking, weaving, sewing and cleaning. Whenever possible I helped Uncle. I was more comfortable outside in the June heat. Being around the animals made me think of Gilbert. I missed him with every minute that passed. Oh how he would have loved those squealing pigs! Uncle reminded me of Gilbert. He was so caring when he tended the animals.

On my third day, Uncle sent me to Proctor's Brook. It was a small body of water, which would have been called a burn back home, that ran along the northeastern edge of Uncle and Aunt Orlie's property. The gurgling water sounded just like the burns that ran off the River Coe in the glen. Water was very important in the Highlands. Not just for drinking and washing. We used water to make healing lotions and protect us from evil spirits that could not cross it. Water was essential to life in Scotland and being near it calmed me. Merlin landed on a nearby branch and rested on his right leg. I sat on the edge, pulled off my boots and dipped my feet in the cool rushing water.

I stayed as long as I dared before pulling my boots on and getting back to work. On my way back from Proctor's Brook with two buckets of water, I heard Uncle yelling.

"Unbelievable!"

Fear seared through my belly at his word. Had I dallied too long at the water? Was Uncle angry with me? I quickened my steps to arrive at Uncle's side earlier. Some of the water stayed in the buckets.

"This is not what I had hoped for," Aunt Orlie said. It was then that I knew they were not talking about me. My fear eased a bit. But clearly, something was wrong.

"The ministers get around to speaking out about the witchcraft trails and this is what they say. Convictions based on spectral evidence alone is worrisome but we should continue to do so, anyway? What sense does that make? None! It is simply madness!"

"Justin, lower your voice. If anyone hears how upset you are, they could accuse you of something."

Uncle muttered something I am certain I was not supposed to hear as I emptied the water into a low trough for the pigs.

"When I was in town early today, looking at a copy of the ministers' letter, I heard someone say that at least no one had been executed on spectral evidence alone."

"What about the woman they hung the day I arrived, ma'am?" I said the words before the thought had formed in my mind. I should not have spoken so freely.

My aunt and uncle exchanged a look. Uncle nodded and Aunt Orlie explained.

"Bridget Bishop was executed the day you came to Salem. They had more evidence than a child's accusation. She was having work done on her cellar and the men found poppets hidden in the walls." Seeing my confused expression, she explained. "It is believed that people who practice black magic can injure others by putting pins in dolls called poppets. Since Bridget Bishop was not of the highest moral character and had been tried but not convicted of witchcraft years ago, these poppets were the final evidence needed to condemn her. Imagine, executed for having forgotten old dolls?"

Poppets? The English had funny words for some things.

"Burns thinks they will stop short of executing anyone solely on words with no proof."

"Hush, now, Justin. Someone comes."

Aunt Orlie turned on her leather heel and retreated into the house. She was a kind woman but only spoke with neighbors when it was necessary. I longed to stay out in the sunshine but knew I could not. The cloth for my new clothes needed more work and it was time for more English lessons. I followed Aunt Orlie in the house.

We were finishing my first recitation of the Lord's Prayer as Uncle burst through the front door.

"Justin. What is it?"

"That was Burns who had just come from Boston. Dr. Toothaker died in the gaol there today. Why was he in jail?"

"Three of the girls accused him of witchcraft."

"On what proof was he held?"

"Their word alone, I believe."

"And I believe the first victim of spectral evidence has been sacrificed."

Chapter Twenty-Five

With few interruptions, life in Salem was quiet. Except when we went to town. When we were on the farm, working, eating and reading lessons I could forget about everything that was happening around our little property. Occasionally, someone would stop by with news, to gossip or to do business with my uncle. Aunt Orlie did her best to keep me hidden without being obvious about it. There was always a chore to be done elsewhere when someone arrived.

My first public visit was to the meetinghouse for church. I wore my new clothes, which dusted the ground as I walked. By then the gossips had spread all over that the Coopers had a new relative living with them. The stories about who I was and how I arrived varied but were always wrong. Uncle and Aunt Orlie did not bother to correct anyone. They only said they were pleased to have me.

The children of Salem were quiet and well behaved in front of the adults. No one my age or younger spoke without being spoken to, at least not when there were older people near. Some of the girls gave me strange, questioning looks, stealing glances out the sides of their eyes while Reverend Parris gave his sermon. None of them smiled at me.

At home on the farm, Uncle read the lessons in the mornings and the evenings and Aunt Orlie helped me follow along in her bible. Sometimes we talked about what the words meant. Reverend Parris barely talked about the lessons at all. He lectured on Salem's current scourge, the witches among us. He told us that we had to repent and reminded us of what horrors awaited us if we did not.

My question was, repent for what? The ones who needed to repent where the witches, not the people they were hurting. If they had called on the devil for help, I doubt they would repent. I tried not to shift in my seat when the Reverend looked my way.

Uncle, Aunt Orlie and I headed for home after services when a man waved his hat to get Uncle's attention.

"Mind yourself, Dory," Aunt Orlie whispered when we stopped to wait for the man to catch up to us. Her reminder grated me a bit, as I had never spoken out of turn in front of others since her instructions.

"Quite a sermon, today, did you not think?" the man asked Uncle. Behind him was a girl about my age. Her dark hair peeked out from under her white bonnet a bit at her temples and her eyes were a strange green color. She looked at me as if she was judging a cow or a chicken at the marketplace. Sizing me up, my father would have said. I studied the dirt on the hem of my new skirt.

"Aye, quite a sermon indeed." I could tell by his voice that Uncle did not agree.

"Yes, well, I wanted my Morgan here to meet your new boarder." He nodded toward me.

"Dory is my niece, Mr. Jequeth, not a boarder."

"Apologizes, ma'am. I meant no disrespect. I know how lonely it can be in a new town for young people and I thought the Christian thing to do would be to introduce your niece to someone her own age. Morgan, say hello."

"Hello." The icy tone in her voice made wish I had worn the wool cloak that hung in the attic where I slept. I picked up my head and looked her in the eyes.

"Hello." I replied, reminding myself to speak in perfect English. In the glen, if someone had dared spoken to me in that tone, I would have returned the greeting with an even icier one. There I had my father, grandfather, and friends to back me up. Here, I did not know what would happen if I was rude, even in the face of rudeness.

"Thank you, Malcolm," Uncle said. "It will be nice for Dory to know someone when we come to services."

"And the trials, of course. There will be trials again next week. Some of Morgan's friends have been summoned to testify. It is a terrible time in Salem."

"A terrible time indeed," Uncle said.

This Mr. Jequeth seemed to be happy that his daughter's friends were involved in the witch trials. Strange. I would think it would concern him, not make him proud.

The adults said their good-byes while Morgan and I continued to eye each other. She would not be my friend. Her circle of friends would not be nice to me either. That was fine with me. I preferred to spend time with the pigs.

It was not until we were in the house that anyone of us spoke.

"Imagine, bragging that he knows girls who will testify against innocent people!" Aunt Orlie said. "I would not be surprised if he remembers being pricked by one of the accused. He seems to want the attention."

"Calm down, now Orlie. Perhaps we should not attend the trials. I do not wish to see you this upset."

"I must attend. I promised Rebecca Nurse that I would speak for her."

"What?" I jumped at the sound of Uncle raising his voice. It made me want to shrink down inside myself to hide. It seemed Aunt Orlie had not told Uncle about her plan. "How could you do such a thing? We agreed to stay out of it."

"That was before anyone had been executed. I cannot stay quiet while an innocent woman is put to death. It would be like killing her myself."

"It may be killing yourself. You know that others who have gone against the tide of accusations have been accused themselves. Many are languishing in horrid conditions in the gaols as far away as Boston. We cannot get involved."

"And if it was me in one of the gaols waiting for trial, would you not expect our friend Goody Nurse to proclaim my innocence?"

Uncle's face turned bright red but he said nothing. Instead, he went outside to feed the pigs. Aunt Orlie got to work on the next meal. I did not like that my aunt and uncle were fighting. I hated that they were fighting about the witch trials. Aunt Orlie was trying to stand by her friend and Uncle was trying to protect her, his wife. They were both right. I did not know what to do about any of it. For the first time in a long time, I was glad to be a child whose opinion did not matter.

"We need water, Dory. Do not linger too long, your uncle will be hungry when he comes in for supper."

I grabbed the two wooden buckets by the fire and headed outside. Uncle must have been in the barn because I did not see him by the pigs. Merlin appeared on a nearby branch and flew from tree to tree along my path to the water.

As I walked, I thought more about their argument. Uncle was right to fear what would happen to Aunt Orlie if she testified in defense of an accused witch. What Aunt Orlie said was right, too, though. She had to do the honorable thing and stand up for her innocent neighbor. It was what we did in the glen.

A twig snapped. I stood still and listened. The sound came from a few yards away, maybe even on the other side of the burn. A snapping twig was not usually a sound to be concerned about but this was louder than normal. The animal that broke that twig was not a squirrel or rabbit. It was much larger, perhaps a deer. Or a human.

Chapter Twenty-Six

All I heard were the thumping of my own heart and the whoosh of my breath. Even Merlin sat silent and still. Had I imagined it? Then I saw movement out of the corner of my eye. A dark figure wearing light colored clothing that was not like any I had seen.

It was a girl, I think. She looked as frightened to see me as I was to see her.

"He-e-llo?" I said.

The figure turned and ran. She was so fast I though she must be part deer.

Remembering Aunt Orlie's warning not to linger, I dunked the buckets in the water and hurried back to the house. With my aunt and uncle already cross with each other, I decided not to tell them about my encounter at the burn. It would cause more trouble.

The tension lasted all week. They never spoke of it again in front of me but I knew that Uncle did not want Aunt Orlie to testify at the trials and Aunt Orlie was not going to heed him. Aunt Orlie continued my English lessons, I still had to recite the Lord's Prayer in order to sit down to a meal. We also continued to spin and weave, as new clothing and linen were always needed.

Sunday came and we went to the meetinghouse as usual. Reverend Parris banged his fist on the wooden pulpit as spittle flew from his lips along with the ominous warnings about evils and evildoers. People fidgeted in their seats as he went on about consequences and the virtues of living a pure life.

After services, my aunt and uncle were trapped in a few conversations about the trials that were to take place the next day. Most of the people confirmed that they intended to stand up for Goody Nurse, an elderly woman who had been kind to all, it seemed.

"How anyone could believe that she would hurt a soul is beyond me," one woman said. All the ladies in the circle agreed and nodded.

One question bothered me. If everyone agree that Goody Nurse could not have hurt anyone, then how did she wind up on trial? The town had laws, right? The sheriff could not just arrest someone for no reason. I did not ask my question, though. It was best for me to be silent on the subject.

The following day, people packed the meetinghouse. In the front was a large table with men sitting behind it, the judges. In the front pew sat five women. Across the aisle from the five women was a group of twelve girls around my age. I recognized Morgan Jequeth among them.

Four of the accusers spoke against Rebecca Nurse. They claimed that Goody Nurse pinched and pricked them and tried to make them sign their names in a book. Other people spoke of seeing Goody Nurse torment the girls.

"Does anyone else who wishes to speak?"

Silence at first. I looked around as best I could without moving my head too much. Finally, a hand was raised, then another. Soon dozens of hands were raised.

"We have a petition of some forty names claiming Goody Nurse has done no harm to them or anyone they know and they do not believe her to be guilty of the current charges against her."

A man brought forward the petition and the judge put it on a pile of other papers without glancing at it. Person after person stood to give testimony to the virtuous and generous character of Goody Nurse. The men of the jury listened as each person spoke. The girls in the front pew sat without so much as a twitch of their hands. Aunt Orlie spoke about Goody Nurse's good nature and the excellent reputation of her entire family.

"Jury, it is your duty to consider all that you have heard today and render a verdict when ready."

The men were led out of the room. The air in the meetinghouse was quite warm so many people left the building. Aunt Orlie, Uncle and I joined them. The accusing girls stood in a circle together, their backs facing out. Morgan Jequeth stared at me, and then whispered something to the group. They all turned to see me.

The sweat on my arm near froze from fear. I had done nothing to these girls. In fact, the only time I had spoken to any of them was when Morgan's father introduced us. What could they have against me that they would stare at me that way? Was it just that I was new? Did they know I was from the Highlands? I tried not to look in their direction.

We were called back into the room when the verdict was ready.

Not Guilty.

The crowd released a huge sigh of relief. Uncle smiled at Aunt Orlie. The madness in Salem was over. On spectral evidence alone, the jury did not convict Goody Nurse.

"We the Court urge you to reconsider this verdict," one of the judges said.

The mood in the crowd changed from relief to confusion. Can he do that?

"We urge you to review the testimony of the accused herself. What have you to say about this Goody Nurse?"

The whispering quieted. Goody Nurse made no response.

"I think we should go out again," one juror said. A few more agreed. They were led out again.

"I do not think she heard them ask her a question," Aunt Orlie said. "She is quite hard of hearing or may be too shocked to move. We must make them be sure she understood them."

"No more. You had to speak up when you were sure of the circumstances. We do not know for sure that is what has happened here."

"We must make sure."

"At the risk of being accused and convicted ourselves?"

Aunt Orlie could not answer that question. The jury came back and read a new verdict.

Guilty.

Rebecca Nurse was led away, back to jail.

Aunt Orlie stood up and left the meetinghouse before the trials of the other women started. Uncle and I followed her out. Dozens of others joined us. Not only had the judges urged the jury to change the verdict, which they did, it all happened without making sure the accused understood what was happening. There was no use in staying to see the others convicted. It was clear. Once you were accused, you had to either confess or be convicted.

Fear, dread and pain for the elderly woman filled my stomach. None of us ate much at the evening meal. Uncle read from the scriptures and then continued to search the book until long after I had gone upstairs to bed. I prayed he would find an answer.

Chapter Twenty-Seven

It rained for three straight days. One night it hailed for more than an hour. Even though their own main crop, pigs, would not be affected by the summer storms, Uncle and Aunt Orlie worried about their neighbors' crops. The previous year's harvest had been water logged and infected with fungus. If this year's crops are bad, the town could go hungry this winter. They wondered during our scripture readings if the rain was Providence showing displeasure in how the town was reacting to the witch accusations. A reminder of how he cleansed the earth of wickedness with the Great Flood in the time of Noah.

A few days after the rain stopped Aunt Orlie came outside while I finished feeding the pigs. We had both been spending more and more time doing outside chores with Uncle and the animals. Aunt Orlie encouraged me, saying she thought it was good for my lungs to be in the sun. My health had improved quite a bit during my time in Salem.

"Dory, get me a nice long stick."

A stick? What had I done wrong? In the glen when a child was told to get a stick or a switch, the adult hit the child with it as a punishment. I stood frozen, knee deep in wriggling pigs, trying to remember what I had done wrong.

"Of course, if you do not wish to learn to write, you do not need a stick."

"Aye, ma'am."

I still did not understand why I needed a stick to learn to write but it was better than being punished so I set out for the closest tree, looking for a good-sized stick that had fallen beneath it. Merlin sat in the tree but ignored me. He only followed me to the water. I called to him a few times when I was sure no one was around at the water's edge. He did not come immediately but when he was ready, he appeared by my side.

"Get two!" Aunt Orlie called out.

Two. Fine, no problem. Excitement built up in my body. I was going to learn to write. True it was writing with a stick, but still. It did not take long before Aunt Orlie and I stood side by side, each with stick in hand, looking at a patch of dirt.

"We will begin with the most important word to you, your name. For a 'D' draw a straight line down, then a curve going to the right. Like a bow."

Aunt Orlie drew as she spoke.

D

"Now, you try."

I knew how to speak so many languages and I could recognize some letters and words in English now, but to be able to form those letters by my own hand was something I never thought I would do. I put my stick on the dirt and drew a line. It wobbled more than Aunt Orlie's did, but it was a line. Then I pictured an archer in my head and drew the curve next to the line.

D

"Good." Aunt Orlie dragged her foot across her letter. The stick marks disappeared and it was a patch of dirt again. She started on the next letter.

"An 'o' is a circle." She ran her stick around in a quick circle

o

I was reluctant to scratch out my first letter. It was the first letter I had ever drawn, but it was time to move on to the second one. I did what my aunt had.

"Fine. The 'r' is a smaller line with a little hook." She drew one, I copied it.

r

"And the 'y' is a small line on a slant to the right and big line on a slant to the left." Again, she drew and I copied.

y

"Now we write them next to each other." She drew each letter without scratching the one before it.

Dory

I put my stick to the dirt and said the letters to myself. The archer, the circle, the line with a hook, the two slanted lines.

Dory

Again, mine was a little shakier than Aunt Orlie's was but it was there. My name. I was proud of it.

"Fine. Now scratch it out and try it again." Scratch it out? It was my name, how could I scratch it out? Aunt Orlie waited. There was plenty of dirt on the farm, was there nowhere else we could practice? In the end, I had no choice. I did as she said, scratched out the letters and wrote them again. We did this over and over until I lost count how many times.

"That will do for now. Tomorrow you will learn to link them together in a signature."

Uncle came over to where we were working when Aunt Orlie was speaking. "Dory you must think upon something very important this evening. When you learn to sign your name, you need a last name as well. You may use MacIain, your family name or MacDonald as it is the name of your clan or you may use Cooper."

"Cooper?" I asked.

"It is a good name," Uncle said. "My family is respected and we have a good reputation in Massachusetts. We would be proud to have you."

"How can I take your name? If my father sends for me, no one will know who I am."

"Your father cannot send for you, child."

He spoke with confidence and sincere regret. I knew he believed what he was saying.

"Why do you say that?" I asked.

"There are those in Scotland who believe you are a fugitive. If your father writes to you, the government may find you and take you to prison. He cannot write. At least, not for many years."

I stood stock-still for a moment and thought about what he said. I was cut off from my family in Scotland. Everything I had was here on this dusty farm in this strange town where people believed witches were pinching little girls.

"Do not answer today, child," Aunt Orlie said after a few moments of silence. "It is a big decision."

I nodded my head. "Aye, ma'am."

It was a big decision. I thought about it through the rest of my chores. I burnt the side of the cornbread because I was paying more attention to my thoughts than the baking. I ate the burnt part. It was still delicious. The problem of choosing a last name continued in my mind as I tried to listen to the bible lessons after supper. It was the only thought I had as I put my head down on the bed.

At first, the answer was simple. I had been sent away from Scotland to preserve the MacDonald way of life, to make sure that MacDonalds lived on forever. What if Uncle was wrong and Father did send for me to come back to Scotland? Would he be able to find me if I took another name? Would it offend him that I took another name? Uncle John, the new chief, had told me to remember that I was a MacIain, a Glencoe MacDonald. Then I thought about my mother. She had not been born a MacIain or a MacDonald. She was a MacGregor. If I ever married, I would not be a MacIain anymore. How was that preserving the name? There were loads of families in the clan with a last name other than MacIain or MacDonald.

Then there was what was best for Aunt Orlie and Uncle. They had been generous to take me in and offer me their name. My aunt had told me to be careful not to let anyone know I was from the Highlands. I had seen how dangerous it was in Salem to be singled out as being different. Perhaps it was the safest thing for all three of us if I took the name Cooper.

Thinking about that made my stomach roll over and tie in knots. How could I dishonor my family that way? A name is a legacy, a gift from our ancestors, a gift we are to pass to the next generations. If I had stayed in the glen and married there, my last name would not be passed to my next generation, the name of my husband would. However, the legacy of my clan would be passed down through my memories. Perhaps that was more important. The MacDonalds of Glencoe could live forever as long as I kept the stories, the legacies, and the fireside tales alive in the colonies. No matter what name I wrote next to 'Dory' on a piece of paper.

Right?

Chapter Twenty-Eight

Uncle was pleased the next morning when I told him my decision. I would be Dory Cooper. Aunt Orlie nodded then said we would practice writing my new last name if there was time before supper. I do not know what my mother and father would have wanted me to do but with all the madness in Salem, it was safest to belong somewhere, at least on paper. In my heart, I still belonged to the clan.

The next few hot weeks of the summer, we did our chores, read our bible lessons and I learned to read and write English starting with my new name. We went to the meetinghouse to listen to the sermons, of course. Morgan Jequeth was always there and never smiled. At anyone, not just me. She sneered from time to time. Ann Putnam, Mary Walcott, Abigail Williams, Mercy Lewis and the other girls seemed to follow Morgan's lead. Adults stayed away from them. I overheard someone tell Aunt Orlie that a servant girl for a local doctor had not done a single chore since all this witchery had started. An exaggeration to be sure, but the idea was clear. The accusing girls had a new power over the townspeople and they were using it.

Back at the house, my favorite time every day was fetching water from Proctor's Brook. Merlin would always know when to appear and follow along the path with me. Except for that one time after the trial for Goody Nurse, I did not see anyone else there. I came to think of it as mine, a place where I did not have to hide who I was. I soaked my hot feet in the cool water and told MacDonald tales to Merlin, in Gaelic and sometimes French if the story called for it. I even sang a few times, although Merlin flew away when I did.

One afternoon I was enjoying my time at the burn, telling Merlin a story about the great Robert the Bruce when I heard an unusual noise.

I concentrated my stare across the water. I knew what to look for this time, not a deer or larger animal, but a person, a dark skinned girl in light colored clothes.

We locked eyes. It was not a girl but a boy. He had thick dark hair but he was definitely a boy. This time I did not speak and he did not run. I could see that his clothes were made of animal hide, not woven cloth like mine. In the glen, we wore a combination of both. That was why they looked different.

"Parlez-vous français?"

I was too shocked to speak at all for a moment. This boy was asking me if I spoke French. In French!

"Oui." I told him I did and asked how he knew. He confessed that he often hid in the woods nearby on his side of the water, listening to my stories.

We talked for a few minutes across the sound of the gurgling burn. He called himself a Wabanaki and asked if I had magic.

"Mais, non!" Of course not, I told him.

Horrified he would tell someone I was a witch, I turned to run. He called out an apology. Something in his voice made me stop. Through stumbling French with a few words I did not understand he explained how his elders warned of witches in the town called Salem. Since I talked to birds and the birds obeyed me, he thought I was a witch. I remembered Aunt Orlie and Uncle's warnings about birds and witches.

I told the Wabanaki the buzzard had been trained by a friend of mine and not very well either, as he did not obey most of the time.

Awk! Merlin protested.

The boy and I laughed. It was getting late and I had to get back. We promised to meet there again. We also promised not to tell anyone that we had seen each other. His elders and my aunt and uncle would not approve of us being friends.

I walked back to the farm, smiling. I had a friend. My first real friend since my best friend died. Alas, I could not share my good news.

When Aunt Orlie told me a visitor was joining us for supper, I was surprised. When I found out it was Reverend Lewis, I was stunned. There were two Reverend Mathers, father and son. Both had signed the letter that was published soon after I arrived in Salem. Reverend Lewis was a close friend to both.

"Why is he coming, ma'am?" I asked as we prepared the meal.

"Your uncle's family is distant relation to the Lewis family. Since he is in the area, there is a mild family obligation."

"In truth, the Reverend enjoys your aunt's stew," Uncle said.

The man who arrived at our door was not wicked looking. He wore the customary black clothes of a reverend but the darkness did not spread to his face. He smiled quite often, especially when Uncle gave him a second helping of stew.

I was silent the entire time Reverend Lewis was in the house. It was the first meal I had without reciting the Lord's Prayer first, which struck me as funny, not having to pray with the reverend in the house. The adults managed to speak about all manner of happenings in Massachusetts before coming around to the witch trials.

"Reverend Mather believes it better for ten suspected witches to go free than for one innocent person to be condemned. I agree with that sentiment fully."

Then why was the exact opposite taking place? Aunt Orlie and Uncle were in a terrible situation. They could not press him for an answer to that question for fear they could be seen as standing up for witches. That would put them at risk of being accused. Did Reverend Lewis not have enough influence over the trials or did he not believe what he was saying to my aunt and uncle? Both could not be true. Did he not possess the power to end the trials or the will? I wondered if there was a way to push him into doing something. If so, who could push him?

Chapter Twenty-Nine

On Saturday, the 19th of July, Rebecca Nurse and four other women were hanged as witches. Many townspeople were witness to it. Uncle, Aunt Orlie and I stayed home and did our normal chores. Then we spent extra hours with our bible lessons and prayers. We did not find answers to the horrible confusion. It was a wicked day for Salem.

Accusations, examinations, trials and testimony continued through August. Five more of the accused were convicted and hanged as witches. Four of them were men. There were many more accused people in the gaols in Boston and other towns. Those who had confessed to being witches had not been hanged. Instead, they suffered in prison until the authorities could figure out what to do with them. It seemed that confessing to being a witch was the only way to keep from being hanged as one. Even if it meant living in jail. The gaols were so crowded that the sheriff released some of those who confessed with the understanding that they could be brought back at any moment.

Uncle and Aunt Orlie were determined to stay away from the witch trials. They were concerned for the town and everyone in it but knew that speaking out against the trials would be disastrous. Instead of cramming into the meetinghouse with their neighbors, they worked together, getting the farm ready for winter. They chopped firewood, picked and gathered the fruits and vegetables and prepared to bring the pigs to market.

The gossip was impossible to escape. People continued to stop by the house with news about recent witch trial happenings and talked to my aunt and uncle after services.

"Rumor is that someone else died in a Boston gaol last week but no one knows for sure who it was," a neighbor told Uncle one afternoon at the meetinghouse.

"The Sheriff has taken to seizing the property of accused witches before they are convicted," another neighbor reported. "There is even a story of him blackmailing the families of the accused, demanding money so that he would not sell their property right out from under them. It is shameful."

All we wanted was to be left alone on our farm to do our work and to be good neighbors. The witchcraft threat consumed so much of people's time they ignored chores on their own farms and in their own businesses. Uncle would offer to help with harvests but neighbors told him they would need his help later. The trials took over the town. Standing in the yard at the meetinghouse in the hot August sun, it looked like there was no escape.

Morgan Jequeth and her friends stood in their circle after services that afternoon. Every few moments, one of them would come over and say hello to me. Just 'Hello, Dory.' I would return in kind. They would run back to the circle and whisper. It made me very nervous. I tried not to look but my eyes kept glancing over at them. What was their problem with me? Did they not trust anyone not in their circle?

Later that afternoon, I ventured a question. I did not like to talk about the trials with Aunt Orlie but the deeds of the sheriff confused me.

"Why is the sheriff taking the lands of the accused, ma'am?"

"You should not be listening to the conversations of adults," she scolded. I bowed my head in regret. She took a deep breath and continued. "The property of convicted witches is awarded to the king. The sheriff takes control of it in his stead. It shames and punishes the family of the witch. What is happening now is wrong, though. He is taking control of property before it is legal for him to do so. There is even thought that he is keeping some of the takings for himself."

"Why will no one stop him?" I pushed.

"He has powerful family members including some of the judges. How can anyone stop him?"

I wanted to say the judges should stop him. Being granddaughter to the chief had let me get away with a few more bad acts in the glen than others my age but my grandfather would never have protected me if I cheated people out of what was theirs. What was wrong with the judges that they could not tell right from wrong? It was difficult but I said nothing further because I had already pushed Aunt Orlie with my other questions. She did not like discussing the trials, especially with me.

We went back outside to work on my writing lessons. My signature had gotten quite good over the weeks. It still seemed strange to scratch out 'Cooper' after 'Dory' but then again I did not know what it was like to write my name the old way.

"We will move on to charcoal, soon," Aunt Orlie said. "It is a little bit more like writing with a pencil or quill pen."

"Yes, ma'am." I wanted to know when I would get to use paper but knew that would be a long time off. Paper was expensive and it did not make sense to use it for practice.

Aunt Orlie looked out over the horizon as if she were enjoying the last heat of the summer. It was unusual to see Aunt Orlie be still. She always had a chore to do. I enjoyed the quiet moment and stood with her. She leaned over to me and whispered.

"Would you like to see your name in Gaelic?"

Her question surprised me. She never let us speak in Gaelic for fear someone might overhear us.

"Aye, ma'am."

Aunt Orlie scratched out the letters of my name in Gaelic. There were eight and the 'o' had an accent. D — e - ó - i — r — i — d — h. Deóiridh.

It was beautiful. Breath caught in my throat for a moment as I looked at it. My parents have given me that name. Now Mother was dead and I had no idea what had become of Father. My name was one of the few things that still connected us. I swallowed hard and lifted my stick to copy my name. Just as my shaking hand touched the stick to dirt, Aunt Orlie straightened her back.

"Hurry," she said as she began kicking dirt onto my name and scratching the ground with her stick. "Someone is coming. They must not see this."

In seconds, I heard what Aunt Orlie must have. The sounds of a wagon headed our way. As much as it pained me, I joined in covering up my Gaelic name. I was still so grateful Aunt Orlie had shown it to me, even if was just for a moment.

I vowed to write it by my own hand as soon as Aunt Orlie thought it was safe. Tears formed in my eyes for the first time in many months. The first time when anyone could see them, anyway. Aunt Orlie and I went inside as Uncle dealt with the visitors.

Any time someone came to the house or Uncle returned from town, I hoped there would be word from the glen. Father could only send for me if the threat against the clan was gone. As King William and his bride Mary continued to reign and the orders to attack the glen came from them, the threat was constant. Still, I could not keep myself from hoping.

"Will this curse ever leave us?" Uncle said as he came through the door.

"What is it, Justin?" Aunt Orlie asked. She put down the knife she used to cut potatoes for our supper. I was washing and snapping beans at the table next to her.

"Burns tells me some of those who have confessed are recanting," he said. He put his hat on the peg by the door and stood still with his arms crossed. "The thought of eternal damnation was too much to bear."

"I do not understand, ma'am," I said.

"Puritans believe that lying causes a separation from Providence,"

Aunt Orlie said. "That separation is an eternal damnation."

"And now these people who had confessed to being witches are saying they made those statements to escape being hanged," Uncle explained. "Now they would rather be hanged with a clear conscience and a path to Providence than to be forever apart from God."

"What will the judges do?" Aunt Orlie asked. "There are more than a hundred people in gaols on witch craft charges. Certainly they will suspend further trials until this can be straightened out."

"That would be logical but nothing in this business has been based on logic so far. They have already executed eleven people and almost half that number have died in prisons awaiting trials. How can the judges admit they made a mistake that led to the deaths of innocent people? This terrible mess is not getting any better."

Chapter Thirty

There was a constant pain in my gut, like I had swallowed an ember and it was burning a slow hole in my belly. Uncle was right about things not getting better in Salem. They were getting worse, much worse. The reverends and judges were going to have to make even more horrible decisions in order to cover up the terrible ones they already made. Or confess that they had no idea what a witch was or how to determine if someone was in league with the devil. I wished I could think of something I could do about it.

My Wabanaki friend came to the water a few days a week. I would tell him highland stories and he would share his people's tales with me. There were hero tales as well as reminder tales about how goodness always wins out over bad. It reminded me of the fires at home. We spoke in French, which was tricky for both of us but we managed. Once he asked me about my necklace. Usually, I kept it tucked under my dress but being at the burn made me freer and I allowed it to glisten in the sun. I told my friend that cairngorms were rare and only came from one set of mountains in Scotland. He told me it was beautiful. He was right.

As I returned to the house with my buckets of water and Merlin flying from branch to branch, a wagon pulled up. Neighbor Burns hopped out and looked around.

"Child, where is your uncle? I must speak with him immediately!"

"I believe he is in the barn, sir."

My worry turned to fear when I heard the tone of his voice. Something was wrong and it concerned Uncle. The man ran to the barn. I followed him, planning to stand to the side of the open barn door so they could not see me as I listened. Aunt Orlie opened the door to the house, having heard the wagon pull up. When she saw me she did what she always did, got me out of the way. She told me to finish emptying the water and get inside to help with supper.

I did as I was told, even though I wanted to hear what was happening in the barn. Had someone new been accused of witchcraft? Or had the judges come to their senses and stopped the trials altogether?

A few minutes passed. Then we heard the wagon pull away and Uncle came into the house. He walked up to Aunt Orlie and looked her in the eyes.

"Bad news, Orlie. Wabanaki have been spotted in the nearby woods."

All the color drained from Aunt Orlie's face. She stumbled a bit and Uncle caught her by the elbow, helping her to stay standing. When she spoke, I could barely hear the words.

"Why are they back?"

"According to Burns, people are saying it's the witchcraft that has brought them because the Wabanaki are in league with the devil, too."

"It is possible." Her voice was so soft I am not sure that was what she said.

"He wanted us to know as soon as possible since we are familiar with how wicked the Wabanaki are."

Wicked? In league with the devil? What were they saying? All this time I thought Aunt Orlie and Uncle were staying away from the trials because they did not believe the charges against the accused. They believed that it took more than one person's wild tale to condemn another. Now it seemed they believed that evil did exist in Salem and that my friend was a part of it.

"They are not evil!" I said before I had a chance to stop myself.

Uncle was across the room and grasping me hard by the arms before I could breathe.

"What do you know of them?" he shouted. He had never shouted before. Ever. To anyone.

"Answer him, child," Aunt Orlie said in her stern voice. "How do you know that name?"

"I...I...," I could not think what to say.

"The truth, Dory," Uncle said. "Now."

"I know one."

He gripped my arms tighter. I feared he would rip them off.

"How do you know one?" he asked through gritted teeth. I glanced to Aunt Orlie, hoping she would get him to let me go. She looked as panicked as he was angry.

"He comes to the burn. We tell each other stories."

"It speaks English?"

"En Français."

Uncle looked confused and turned to Aunt Orlie.

"They speak in French," she translated.

"Did anyone see you?" he demanded. "Tell me, did anyone see you?"

"N-n-no, sir. I don't think so."

His grip did not relax.

"No more, child," Uncle ordered. "No more. I will fetch the water from now on."

"But why? I don't understand!"

"You will do as you are told. Go upstairs, now. Pray to God that he may cleanse you of whatever sin that Wabanaki has cast upon you."

I paused a moment, ready to ask again what I had done to anger them. Aunt Orlie walked across the room and touched her hands on Uncle's. He released my arms.

Confusion and panic drove me from the room. I ran up the stairs as fast as I could. Aunt Orlie and Uncle were acting as if they believed I was in league with the devil. They were more angry than I had ever seen them. Their anger and my sadness over losing my only friend poured out in a furious crying jag that lasted for hours.

The next morning I woke with dried tears on my face and dread in my stomach. The house was silent. Where was Aunt Orlie? Had she gone to town with Uncle to make arrangements to get rid of me? Would they give me back to Captain Harris? Or put me on a different ship going to pirate-infested Barbados?

I could not stay upstairs forever. It was time to find out what would happen to me. On the table downstairs was my breakfast, cornbread and honey mead. That was strange. Although if they wanted someone else to take me, they would have to make sure I seemed healthy. I was not hungry, my stomach filled with dread, but I ate the meal anyway. It could be the last one I saw for a long time. As I wiped off the trench, a wagon pulled up outside. Moments later, Aunt Orlie walked through the front door.

"Good morning, child."

"Morning, ma'am." I kept my head bowed. Even though they were very angry with me, I did not want to leave my aunt and uncle.

"Are you feeling better?"

No.

"Aye, ma'am."

"I see you have eaten already so let's hear the Lord's Prayer now."

The prayer? Why would she care if I could recite the prayer if she was sending me away? Did this mean she was keeping me?

"You remember how it starts, child?"

"Yes, ma'am." I proceeded to recite it without a single stumble.

"Fine. You are a good student, Dory. Your writing is coming along nicely, too."

"Thank you, ma'am." This was quite confusing. Was she still angry with me? Was Uncle?

"Yesterday was unfortunate." She sat at her spinning wheel. I picked up my loom and sat on the stool next to her. "We should have told you how brutal the Wabanaki can be. For years, they raided these parts of the English world. They destroyed property, stole what they wanted and kidnapped or killed anyone they came across. They were trying to gain back land they believe is theirs by scaring the English off of it."

I wanted to protest by saying the one I knew was not a killer but this time, held my tongue.

"You should have told us when you met this boy at the burn. We understand he was nice to you, but he could have been followed by a Wabanaki with death in his heart. It is not safe for you to go to the burn alone. Your uncle will go."

Disappointment must have shown on my face but I said nothing.

"When I first arrived here, being near the water helped me feel less homesick. I think it helps you, too. Perhaps once Justin has chased the boy from the water, you will be permitted to join him. You are a child in our home and we must protect you."

My heart ached for my friend. He would never know that I still wanted to be friends. He would think he offended me. I wished I could go to the water to tell him why I would not return but knew it would not be permitted. Aunt Orlie had said I could stay in their home and that was more important.

"Mary Easty, Rebecca Nurse's sister, is to go on trial tomorrow," Aunt Orlie said. "Justin and I went out this morning to discuss what we should do. Ignoring the problem has not helped. We must go to the trial and see for ourselves what is happening."

Going to the meetinghouse on Sundays was bad enough with the strange way Morgan Jequeth and her friends treated me. Attending another trial would be even worse. Of course, Aunt Orlie was not discussing it with me, she was telling me what we were doing.

"When are we going, ma'am?"

"Today. It will be hot and stuffy in the meetinghouse and you should not be inside all day. Go outside to help your uncle with the pigs."

I lowered the loom to my lap and looked at Aunt Orlie.

"Uncle was so angry with me yesterday, ma'am. He may not want my help."

She took the loom from me.

"It will do both of you good to work side by side in the sun. It will remind you that we are a family, no matter what happens to any of us."

Aunt Orlie was more confident that Uncle would forgive me than I was but I went outside anyway. Being part of a family took work.

The sun was shining bright in the late summer morning. Uncle had already sweated through his shirt as he sloshed buckets of slop into the low wooden pig troughs. The pigs squealed and wriggled as each one fought for its turn. They were so cute, it was hard not to smile.

Uncle stood up and stretched his back. He turned and saw me. I stood still, waiting for him to yell at me again.

"There are two more buckets of slop. Empty them into the trough." His voice did not have its normal warmth but he did not sound angry. He sounded tired.

"Your aunt told you we are going to the meetinghouse today?"

"Aye, sir."

"To think all this started because some girls used an egg to find out who their husbands would be. A silly girl's crush. Ridiculous."

"Sir?" I had heard of an egg yolk in water foretelling a possible husband. The healers sometimes did it on Samhain, the last day of October, for fun.

"These witchcraft accusations started when some girls were caught using the egg yolk in water test. From there, the reverend blew it out of proportion and it keeps getting worse. More than fifteen people have died because of the curiosity of a few girls. See, child, even innocent dealings can lead to disaster."

"Aye, sir." I got his meaning. As mother had told me a little wicked goes a long way. Uncle was also talking about my friendship with a Wabanaki. I wanted to ask if he had seen him when he fetched the water but knew not to push it. His anger was gone for now, but it could return quickly.

"Once the pigs are fed," he said. "Then we will find out how chaotic this has gotten."

Chapter Thirty-One

Tension filled the meetinghouse the way fog filled the glen, it was heavy and found every corner. I realized why Aunt Orlie and I had been helping Uncle with his outside chores so much. Every man and woman I knew from Salem, and dozens I did not, were in this small building. Instead of helping each other with chores, the men were attending the trials. Who was caring for the harvest? No one.

The judges sat at the front with empty seats for the accused on one side, the accusers on the other and the jurors near it all. Uncle stood but found places for Aunt Orlie and me to sit. Between the heat and the crowd of people, the air in the building was enough to make me dizzy.

The doors opened and the sheriff brought in four of the accused. Several people begin to move around in their seats. It was more than fidgeting. Morgan and her friends moaned along with their fits.

A smoldering anger inside me began to grow. What were these girls doing? If sorcerers possessed them, those sorcerers were not in the courtroom. Why would a powerful creature bother pricking girls when there were all kinds of real problems they could cause? None of this made sense. It had to have something to do with Morgan. But what?

During the judges predictable interrogation of Mary Easty, Morgan and her friends alternated fidgeting and sitting as still as stone. I wanted to smack them all, the girls, the judges, the townspeople.

I watched Reverend Parris, sitting in the corner, writing as each person spoke in order to have an official record of the proceedings. It seemed strange to have him do the writing since so many from his household were involved in the trials.

Then something extraordinary happened. Mary Easty suggested to the court, pleaded with the judges, to separate the accusers from one another and ask them one-on-one to tell about their terrors. It was a good idea. The other girls would crumble under a real interrogation without Morgan there to lead them in their strange acts.

However, the judges did not respond to Mary Easty's plea. The sheriff led her from the room. I saw Aunt Orlie and Uncle exchanged a look of fear, which increased my fear and anger both a hundred fold. The other three trials went the same way. One or more of the girls would have a fit or claim she was being pinched and tormented by the accused. Every once in a while, other townspeople in the meeting-house would fall into a fit or say they saw the accused torment one of the girls.

When another one of the accused argued that it was not her fault if the devil took her form, the judges returned that she must have done something or the devil would not have chosen her. Each of the other three were convicted and sent back to jail to await their execution.

Coming to town to see the chaos for ourselves had not done anything to make me feel better. These people were obsessed with the idea that the devil was among them, using their own neighbors. But, there was no proof. Adding to the confusion were those who were recanting their witch confessions. Mary Easty's idea of separating the accusers had merit but the judges refused to listen. How would this ever come to an end?

When the meetinghouse emptied, I filed out into the sun with Aunt Orlie and Uncle. Adults gathered in groups.

"We are fortunate that the judges are discharging wickedness from our town," I heard one man say. Others in his group nodded in agreement.

The group Aunt Orlie and Uncle were in was much quieter. They were observing more than speaking.

"What do you think of our town, Dory?"

I was surprised to hear someone talking to me. It was Morgan Jequeth. She pronounced my name 'Door-eeee' to annoy me, I was sure.

"I am happy to be living with my aunt and uncle," I told her.

"For certain. Afterall, you are the same kind of person as your auntie."

"What do you mean by that?" Suspicion pricked at the hairs on the back of my neck.

"Oh, I think you know. Good-bye, Door-eeee."

I did not know what she was talking about but I knew it was bad news for me. Morgan did not like me. The reason, whether it was that I did not beg to be part of her circle of girls or because I was an outsider, did not matter. She could make up any lie she wanted and accuse me of being a witch. The sheriff would take me to jail. My safe home with my aunt and uncle would be gone and I would bring shame to their name. How could I stop that from happening?

Supper chores awaited us when we arrived home. I got to work on the biscuits. Aunt Orlie and Uncle shared a drink before getting to work. It was unusual for them to drink rum except with meals. Morgan's veiled threat weighed on my mind. I had to get more information from Aunt Orlie.

"Ma'am, why do people accept that the devil has turned their neighbors into evildoers? Do they not believe in the goodness of their friends?"

"They believe these witches are a punishment from God. Puritans are never good enough to please God so when something bad happens – crops fail, Indians attack, witches infest the community – they believe they brought it on themselves as retribution from an unhappy Lord."

"That is odd thinking, is it not? Bad luck happens, good people fall ill or are struck down by enemies. It may be a test but never a punishment. Tell me you do not believe as they do."

"We are not like those people, Dory but we must fit in. Up until this witch trial business, this was a safe, hard-working community, even with the separation between farmers and merchants. We have to believe the hysteria will pass and we can again be safe here. But we must not stand out. We must not draw undo attention to ourselves. Be pious and most importantly, be invisible."

Be invisible. With Morgan Jequeth watching me whenever I was near her, I did not think trying to be invisible would keep me safe.

Chapter Thirty-Two

The fear and suspicion Morgan raised at the meetinghouse stayed with me. I tried to understand how the adults in the community had allowed themselves to be taken in by these girls. Then again, I feared Morgan and her friends and yet had no evidence that they would hurt me or anyone else.

Morning and evening prayers became more solemn in our house. Before we used the words for my English lesson, we discussed what the words meant to us in our lives, how we could use the Lord's words to protect us from the terrible situation in Salem.

Uncle fetched all the water that week. I missed my friend. I also missed Merlin. Without my trips to the burn, he was not around as much. Once in a while, he perched in the tree above the pigs. He enjoyed making them squeal at the sight of him.

Sunday morning dawned and we gathered our things to go to the meetinghouse. My plan was to stay close to Aunt Orlie so Morgan or any of the other girls could not speak to me without an adult overhearing. It was not a great plan, but it was all that I had.

Reverend Parris continued his rant about evildoers and the consequences of letting the devil into your life. In Salem, ministers had more authority than the judges did. As long as he and the other local ministers believed the devil was at work, the trials would continue.

After services, one of the neighbors led Aunt Orlie and Uncle away from the group. I could not follow. Morgan took her opportunity.

"Do you have any devil-worshiping friends, Dory?" Morgan asked, inching ever closer.

"What are you talking about?"

Morgan whispered in my ear.

"I saw you talking with that Indian. In a strange language. Were you making plans to meet with the devil?"

I could feel my eyes widen and my stomach drop. A horrible taste filled the back of my mouth. Morgan must have been the one who reported seeing the Wabanaki. Why had she not turned me in to the authorities already? What did she want from me?

"What is it with your family and the heathen Indians?"

"What rubbish do you speak?" I tried to hide the fear in my voice with anger but it was difficult to do with a whisper.

"Margaret, the daughter of your aunt and uncle, of course. If she had not been so close to Indian Territory, she would be alive today. What was she doing there, Dory? Running an errand for the devil?"

Fear and confusion boiled up in my chest.

"What are you saying about Margaret?" Aunt Orlie and Uncle always spoke about her as if she were married and living elsewhere, like their sons. If she was dead, why would they keep her death from me?

"She was killed in a Wabanaki raid. Not even two years ago. Here is the real question, why was she there? Was she at a meeting with the devil?"

I could not trust that Morgan was telling me the truth. Why would she lie? What was she after? How she could make my head spin with her words!

"Why should you say such vicious things about my cousin? What proof do you have that she had anything to do with witchcraft?"

A laugh gurgled out of her mouth. "Proof? Have you not been paying attention? Proof is what the others believe."

The truth of her statement stabbed at my heart. I could do nothing but watch as she sauntered back to her circle of friends. Morgan controlled the situation. But how? To what end?

If Margaret had been killed by Wabanaki, no wonder Aunt Orlie and Uncle had acted so severely when I told them of my friendship. They were afraid for my life because of what had happened to their only daughter. But how could I find out if Morgan was telling the truth? Asking my aunt and uncle outright seemed cruel.

That night I had trouble sleeping. I was wearing Margaret's too-short-for-me nightclothes and laying in her bed. When I thought she had grown up and left home, using her things had seemed fine, even natural. If she had been killed by the same Indian tribe that my friend belonged to, it all seemed wrong. My skin itched for the first time since I had gotten off the Raven.

In the next few days, the weather turned cooler and the leaves began to turn to their autumn colors. It was my favorite time back in the glen. Our winter food stores would be full, the sun would warm us during the day but we needed our wool cloaks and plaids at night as we sat by the fire. The colors from the leaves reflected off the lochs making it seem like the banks were flaked with gold. It was beautiful. I missed it. The leaves were changing in Salem but there were no nighttime fires or telling of clan tales. It was not the same. To make matters worse, the food stores were not full as the harvest was not all in, although it should have been.

With the extra questions about Margaret on my mind, I faltered with my chores a bit, burning another batch of cornbread. I even stumbled while reciting the Lord's Prayer before supper one night. Aunt Orlie was not happy. She made me repeat it three times before I could to eat.

"There is another trial tomorrow," Uncle said as we ate the potato leek soup Aunt Orlie and I had made. "There is talk that more people are recanting their confessions. The ministers and judges having trouble sorting through it all."

"That is the best reason to halt the proceedings at once," Aunt Orlie said. "We need to work as a community to figure this out, not turn against ourselves. The whole business breeds suspicion."

"We have to attend the trial tomorrow."

"I agree. There must be an end."

I did not sleep well that night. After I was sure Aunt Orlie and Uncle were asleep, I wrapped myself in Margaret's red cloak and crept down the stairs and outside. I did not venture but a few steps from the door. The crisp air felt wonderful against my face and filling my lungs. There had to be a way out of this witch trial mess. The judges and ministers had to be made to see that while they meant to be doing something good, they were hurting the community. Who could convince them? Many had tried and some had died for their efforts.

A noise in the nearby trees caught my attention. My heart raced. It was not the pigs, the noise was from further out than that. I waited, staying still. The sound continued from the trees. Suddenly, a creature came out of the woods and flew straight toward me. I opened my mouth to scream when I realized I recognized that creature.

"Merlin!" I whispered a scolding. "Mad bird! You are supposed to sleep at night."

Then again, so was I. I waved at him and headed back to bed.

The next day we went to the trials of four more people. Many gave witness about prickings and visions, just as in the other trials. The judges decided as usual. All four would be executed in five days along with the four from the previous week. Eight more lives.

I did my best to get Aunt Orlie and Uncle to leave as soon as the meetinghouse emptied but they wanted to stay and speak with their neighbors. More and more people were speaking out against the trials in private circles, mainly due to the number of people taking back their confessions.

"Why in the big hurry to leave, Door-eeee?" I jumped at the sound of Morgan's voice next to my ear. I had not heard her approach. She appeared as if from the air.

"I have chores to do."

"Your family did not come to the trials until after your aunt and uncle heard about the Wabanaki. Are they teaching you what happens if you sign the devil's book?"

"I learned right and wrong as a child. There is no need to teach me again."

"Do you see what happens to evil-doers? Those witches are going to hang for their heresy."

I stared Morgan straight in the eyes. "I know a witch when I see one."

The air between us was like a brewing lightning storm. We were eye to eye for a few silent moments. Then a slow, sneer spread across her face.

"In case you have not heard, so do we."

Chapter Thirty-Three

I rode home in stunned silence. The magnitude of what I had done was slow to sink in to my mind. I had done something about the witch trials, but it was the most reckless thing possible. As soon as we got back to the farm, I went out behind the house and threw up.

Through the rest of the afternoon and supper, I could not look at Aunt Orlie and Uncle. Fear and shame over provoking Morgan raced through my body. What had I done? Again, that night I could not sleep. I waited for the sounds of Uncle snoring then wrapped the cloak around my body and slipped outside. This time I did not confine myself to the front stoop. Instead, I ran to the burn. It could be my last chance to be near water, ever. The night was as dark as ink but I knew my way well. Merlin, who again was not sleeping either, flew along with me.

I flung myself to the ground by the water's edge, panting from the run. I dipped my hand in the water and washed the slick sweat from my face. The tears came, a soft cry at first but before long, I was sobbing. I had done a rash and dangerous thing. Talking to Morgan that way, I had all but dared her to tell on me about talking to the Wabanaki boy. It was bad enough that if she told the ministers or judges I had pinched her from across a room, they would believe her. Morgan had one better. I *had* talked with the Wabanaki, communicated in a language that few in Salem understood. She could accuse me of witchcraft with things I had actually done. Aunt Orlie and Uncle could not protect me.

Eventually I sat up, sitting by the water, listening to it rush over the rocks. A strange calmness came to me, as if all the crying had released me of the past in order to face my future, no matter how short it would be.

I stayed a long, long time by the water. If I was to be taken to the gaols, I could not risk wearing Mother's cairngorm. The sheriff might take it or it could fall off and I would never find it. I did not want it around my neck along with a noose. With sticks and mud, I made a safe place to hold mother's necklace.

Knowing it was possible I would never see my precious gem again, I headed back to the house at a much slower pace. I was a few yards from the water when I heard a noise that did not belong to the night. It was too loud to be an owl or a raccoon. Had my friend come to the burn to look for me? I turned and saw a shadowy figure holding a lit tree branch. Whoever it was had to be on my side of the water.

"Were you expecting your Wabanaki?"

My stomach lurched. Morgan. The flames threw eerie shadows across her face.

"I came to tell you that you will be arrested tomorrow."

I was grateful for the calmness I had gained after my cry. Otherwise, I may have fainted.

"I had hoped you would want to be friends. Your cousin was my friend."

"Aunt Orlie did not tell me that."

"She did not know. Margaret and I were secret friends. Would you like to know why?"

I did not respond.

"That Wabanaki boy, the one you talk to in your strange language? He was my friend, too. Margaret knew some of that language, French, was it? Not as much as you, but enough to talk to the boy. Your aunt taught her how to speak it."

"What wild tales do you tell now?" Only her tale did not sound wild. Aunt Orlie did know French and would have taught it to her daughter. If Margaret had believed Morgan was sincere with her friendship with the boy, she may have helped her.

"It is the truth. He told us stories about his people. They have some strange ideas."

I stayed silent this time.

"I was there the day Margaret was killed. No one knows that, of course. We met at the water as we always did. We left at the same time but Margaret never made it home. Her blood-smeared bonnet lay a few yards from here for your aunt to find. My father said she cried for three straight days."

A horrible thought came to me and I shuttered as it passed through my mind. Had Morgan killed my cousin and let the others believe it was the Wabanaki?

"Why did you not ask me to help you talk to the boy?"

"I was testing you at first, seeing if I could trust you to help me. Before I could figure it out, you were no longer allowed to go to the water."

"Because you told that you saw the Wabanaki. That is your fault, not mine."

"I did not tell. Someone else saw the Wabanaki, in Andover, not Salem. But your aunt and uncle are too scared to let you come here. Now you are of no use to me. I can turn you in as a witch."

Fear was creeping up from my stomach but I tried to think about my new calmness.

"What does that gain you?"

"I get to turn in another evil-doer and gain the gratitude of the ministers and judges."

"This has to end."

"It will. For you."

Her voice was ice cold. It made me shiver as my mind raced. Morgan had been waiting for a chance to get me to help her talk to a boy? A boy she could not speak with by herself. Now that I was banned from the water, she was going to send me to jail to await execution and shame my new family's name.

Mother had said a little wicked goes a long way. How far did a lot of wicked go? I stood still and watched as Morgan's torch faded into the darkness, sparks shooting off it and burning out in the cold air, fearing I would find out.

Chapter Thirty-Four

The sheriff and a local minister came to the house before I was out of bed. Aunt Orlie looked even paler than she had when they found out about the Wabanaki. Uncle was angry.

"We are here for the child," the sheriff announced.

"On what charge?" Uncle demanded.

"Witchcraft."

"That is absurd." Aunt Orlie blurted out. Uncle held up his hand, telling her to be quiet.

"On whose word?" he asked.

"Morgan Jequeth and two others all say her ghostly appearance pinched and otherwise hurt them while trying to get them to sign the devil's book."

What? Morgan made up a charge? If she told them I spoke with the Wabanaki then I would have to confess because it would be true. Why would she make up something else?

"What do you say to these charges?"

Then I understood. If I confessed, I would be saved, or at least stay alive in jail with the hope that I would one day be set free. By falsely accusing me, a confession would be a lie. I had to tell the truth and deny the charges. That meant I would get a trial and be condemned to an execution.

"We obey the Lord in this house." Uncle said.

"Is that so?" the minister asked. "Child, can you recite the Lord's Prayer?"

"Our Father, which art in Heaven, hallowed be thy name. Thy kingdom come, thy will be done in earth as it is in Heaven. Give us this day our daily bread. Forgive us our debts as we forgive our debtors. Lead us not into temptation, but deliver us from evil. For thine is the kingdom, the power, and the glory forever. Amen."

Flawless.

The minister turned to the sheriff. "Perhaps we should examine her further before we take her to the gaol."

"I have orders to take her. That is what I will do."

"You heard her," Uncle protested. "She recited the prayer perfectly. What other proof do you need?"

"Proof is for the court. I have to follow orders."

Aunt Orlie stepped toward me and wrapped her arms around me. It was the first time she hugged me. And would be the last. The sheriff grabbed me by the arms and ripped me from my aunt's grasp.

"Be careful how you treat her, Sheriff. She has not been convicted, yet."

"They are always guilty of something."

I could not look at my aunt and uncle as they took me to the wagon outside and tied my wrists to the side. I could not bear to think of the pain they must feel. I had left my pain by the water's edge.

As the wagon rattled by the tree used for hanging witches, I looked up at it. A large bird stood on one of the branches. It was a buzzard. My buzzard. It was Merlin.

The gaol stunk, literally. Buckets and chamber pots were overflowing with human waste. Dirt covered every surface. People were vomiting everywhere and there was never a moment without the sound of a cough and the wailing of at least one prisoner. The stench overwhelmed me. The conditions were as bad as they had been on the ship with one difference. There was loads of conversation. Everyone had a story to tell and told it to anyone who would listen. I wanted to listen.

Day and night, I heard recanted confessions. People who had given in to the fear of execution and lied about their deeds in order to escape death, now wanted to clear their names before God. The accused were frightened and confused about what to do.

Rumors flew around prison, too. They say it took Giles Corey two days to die. They called him before the court and he refused to go. He would not allow them to question him. The judges took advantage of some strange law that allows the sheriff to tie a man down between two large boards and continue to add heavy rocks on the top board until the man gives a plea to the court. In Giles Corey case, they wanted him to confess being a witch. His only response, "More weight." They continued to add rocks until, two days after they started, Corey had no more breath left to give. He had been pressed to death.

Not including those who died in prison, twelve people had executed for witchcraft since the day I arrived three months ago and eight more on the schedule to hang the next day. How long would this go on? Who was next to be accused? Who was next to die? Me?

Whenever I felt hopeless or sad, I reminded myself about that night at the burn when I left my pain there. Do not feel, just listen and think. I heard loads of people filled with hope that they would be released, that the judges and ministers would come to their senses and stop this madness. Others were sure they were going to die. I kept listening.

I do not know how many days had passed before the jailer called my name. I thought they were taking me to court and was relieved to see Uncle waiting in a small room for me.

"Are you alright, child?" he asked. He held my hands as he spoke.

"I am fine."

"Are they feeding you?"

"The biscuits are hard as rocks and the meat is rancid but I get enough."

We were silent for a while, staring at each other.

"Is Margaret dead?"

Uncle took his hands back as if I had bitten him.

"Why would you ask that?"

"Morgan told me, sir. She said the Wabanaki killed her."

He paused for a moment, as if trying to figure out how to answer me. Finally, he let out a heavy sigh.

"Aye, yes. That is true."

"Uncle, why did you not tell me?"

"It was not a conscious decision. We do not speak of it between ourselves."

"I wore her clothes, slept in her bed, did her chores. You did not think I should know?"

He leaned in close, took my hands again and whispered.

"You must confess."

"What?" My whisper was louder than I meant it to be because I was surprised by his request. "I cannot, Uncle."

"I made a deal with the jailer. If you confess, you can come home with us. It will save him one more person to look after. If you come home, there may be a chance to get you out of Massachusetts. I have family in Virginia."

"They chased one man down in Maine, Uncle. I heard so in here."

"He was the enemy of a powerful family. They would not chase you, I know it."

"My other uncle forced me to run from the English. I do not want to run again."

"You must. It is the only way."

"I may have another way."

"No, child. You must listen to me."

I took my hands from his grasp and laid them on his arms the way he had when he first met me at the docks and the way Aunt Orlie had the night we found out about the Wabanaki.

"Please, Uncle, I cannot run again. There was nothing I could do in Glencoe. I am now a Cooper and part of Salem. This community needs someone to stop the witch trials. It is my duty to try to help them and in so doing, save my own life. I have no doubt that I will die if I fail, but the town is already dying. Please, sir. At least listen to my plan."

He paused for a moment, then agreed.

"Tell me, then. What is it?"

"I have listened to many stories in just a few days. I believe if you can convince one of the ministers, perhaps Reverend Lewis, to come and listen, too. He may put a stop to this."

"Others have tried that plan. He will not come."

"Will he come to hear just one story? Mine?"

Uncle thought for a few moments. "Perhaps I can use my family influence. I hear he has not been feeling well so I will also bring him some of Orlie's headache remedy. In the meantime, consider my suggestion." We were both silent for a moment. "Your aunt would like to hold you again."

As he left, he did not look hopeful.

Chapter Thirty-Five

I concentrated on listening to other people's stories and not on my own thoughts. Although, late at night when the cries were quietest and even the rats took a rest, I wondered if my uncle would be able to get a reverend to come see me. Would he be able to get Reverend Lewis? What would I do if he could not? I knew the answer to that and it was not good. I would die at the hanging tree, branded a witch, shaming the family that had taken me in when they did not have to. Tears leaked from my eyes.

Eight people hanged the next day. The vomiting and crying increased in the gaol. My calmness wavered. Perhaps Uncle would not be able to convince the minister to visit me. Had I failed everyone? Would the MacDonalds of Glencoe stories end with me? Would Aunt Orlie and Uncle suffer through the loss of another young family member who had lived in their home? If I failed, I failed everyone. These people in the gaol would die, either by the court or from the terrible conditions.

The jailer called my name a few days later. Again, I feared it was my turn for a trial. Relief flooded my body when I saw Reverend Lewis sitting next to Uncle at a small table. Anticipation followed relief. The minister was rubbing his temples.

"Your uncle assures me you have something important to say," he stated. "I have known his family for many years and have granted him this favor."

"Thank you, sir," I said. "Sir, I come from the Highlands of Scotland." Uncle cringed as I said it, but what did I have to lose at this point? If I did not convince this man that all the trials were based on false testimony, than we were all condemned. "I know how dangerous a witch can be. One witch foretold the death of my best friend and he died the next day, defending me."

"That may be, child, but all you have told me is that you come from a place where there are witches. That hardly proves you to be innocent."

"Pinching, poking, asking someone to sign a book. These are the charges against most of the people in this gaol, is that right?"

"Yes, yes. Those are the charges," the minister confirmed. He continued to rub his head.

"I am telling you sir that witches are dangerous, wicked creatures who cause true harm. They can kill entire herds of cattle, ruin whole crops and even take the lives of people they dislike. That is the true witchcraft which has occurred here."

"Dory, what are you saying!" Uncle asked with alarm in his voice.

"I must agree with your uncle. That sounded like a confession."

"No, sir. I caused no harm to anyone. Others have." I swallowed hard, then took a breath. "The accusers."

"This is nonsense!"

The minister rose to leave. I had to get him stay. My life, the lives of dozens, possibly hundreds were at stake. The legacy of my clan rested on my next words. I chose them carefully.

"How was the harvest this year?"

The minister paused, his hand still on his head.

"What do you mean?"

"I hear that many people were too occupied with the trials or were jailed themselves and the crops went without water during our dry spell and were not watched during the rain spell. Some were left to rot in the fields as people sat in the meetinghouse. Is this true?"

"Yes. We are trying to buy enough food to feed the town from other towns and we are also asking for donations."

"Do you not see, sir? Lack of food is a true threat. There may be people who starve this winter because of the trials. Who caused the trials?"

"The witches, of course."

"No, sir. The accusers. Not until the people in the Reverend Parris household began accusing people did anything unusual happened. Is that not correct, sir?"

He was silent for a moment, taking his hand from his head. "There were illnesses."

"What happened to those who suffered?"

"They were cured when the accusations began."

"You understand, sir. I make no accusations myself, as I have no proof. I ask that you listen to the people here. They are frightened and some turned away from God in their fear. They wish for you to lead them back to the Lord. They are waiting for you to save them, here and from eternal damnation. Is it not better to set a possible witch free than to execute an innocent person?"

I used the same phrase he had used while sitting at my uncle's table, eating my aunt's stew. We all remembered it. The three of us sat in silence for many moments. The minster looked from me to my uncle. He stood.

"Sheriff!" he called.

Tears sprang to my eyes and my inner calm shattered. Had I failed everyone?

"Sir, please!" Uncle pleaded.

The sheriff came into the room.

"Release this child to her uncle."

Uncle and I looked at each other. Had we heard him correctly?

"I will be speaking with those persons who wish to speak with me in private."

Uncle flung his arms around me and hugged me harder than anyone had in my entire life.

We had done it! We got the reverend to say he would listen to reason. There was still work to be done, but now there was hope. People could tell their stories to someone who would listen and possibly do something about their situations. And I could go home. Uncle did not leave my side as the sheriff let me out of the gaols.

I wanted Morgan arrested for her wicked deeds. Whether she used supernatural powers, the kind Calum feared, or had simply taken advantage of a strange situation and used it to her own gain, I could not prove. I knew in my heart that she had caused the deaths of those innocent people but I had no proof, so to accuse her would be doing to her what she had done to the others. The very thing for which I wanted her condemned. I had to be content that for the first time in many months there was now hope in Salem. And that I was free.

Aunt Orlie was feeding the pigs when we pulled up in the wagon. She looked up, blocking the sun with the back of her hand. As soon as she saw my form on the seat next to Uncle, she dropped her bucket and ran toward us. I jumped down from the wagon. We held each other and cried.

Inside, I washed my hands and feet. It was amazing how filthy my time in jail had made me. I changed out of my dirty clothes into the ones I had worn my first day in Salem. Margaret's clothes.

Aunt Orlie made cornbread as she listened to what had transpired with Reverend Lewis.

"You took quite a chance, admitting you are from the Highlands," she said.

"Aye, ma'am but what choice did I have?"

"You are a crafty lass, aren't you?"

"When I have to be."

We worked together to make a delicious supper and savored every bite. After the meal, Uncle picked up a bucket to fetch the water we would need for the evening.

"May I fetch it?" I asked. It was chancy but they were in a good mood and I wanted to be near the water again.

Aunt Orlie and Uncle looked at each other. Then Uncle answered.

"If you see anyone, Wabanaki or not, run."

"Aye, yes." I took Margaret's cloak off the hook by the door, grabbed the buckets and left before they could change their minds.

Awk! Awk!

"Some help you were," I told him. "You thought they were going to hang me!"

Awk! he protested.

"Quiet before you get me arrested again!" For once, he obeyed.

The water was wonderful. It was full from a recent rain and gurgled along carrying leaves and twigs downstream. After filling the buckets, I reached in and splashed some water on my face. I opened my eyes and saw my reflection staring back at me. I dipped my hand in through my watery image and pulled out a small clay doll, my cairngorm still wrapped around it. The crude doll was made of one twig crossing another where the arms were and mud to fill in the body. It had taken me almost two hours to make it in the shape of Reverend Lewis. The little head had been warn away a bit by the gentle running water, at the temples.

"Thank goodness he let me go when he did. If he had waited many more days, his head would be gone and my plan would never have worked." I untied and unwound the strap for my stone, then tied and retied it around my neck, back where it belonged.

Awk! Awk!

"I know, I know. My clay doll, my corp criadhach, was a little wicked. But what choice did I have?"

A twig snapped. Fear made my legs jittery and my stomach gurgle. What was that? I squinted my eyes and searched across the water. There was my Wabanaki friend. We grinned at each other and waved.

Then I picked up my buckets and ran, as fast as I could, home.

Fact versus Fiction

Historical fiction is fiction sparked by a real person, place or event and then uses fictional characters, places, and events to tell a new story.

The Glencoe Massacre and the witch trial crisis in Salem, Massachusetts both really happened in 1692. There are many different accounts of each of these events, which makes getting to the absolute truth unlikely. Here's what most historians can agree on.

The attack at Glencoe started just before dawn on the 13th of February 1692. It was ordered by King William and carried out by soldiers under Robert Campbell of Glenlyon's command. Thirty-eight people, including the MacIain and his wife, were slaughtered in the small village but many more escaped into the surrounding areas. The wife of the second son of the chief was indeed the niece of Glenlyon.

The hysteria of the Salem witch trials claimed its first victim, Bridget Bishop, on the 10th of June 1692 and ended in September or October, depending on the source. Hundreds of people were accused of witchcraft. Some were hanged, some died from the ghastly living conditions in the jails and one man was pressed to death.

Explore and enjoy the many resources for learning more about the actual events.

Acknowledgements

Even though this is a work of fiction and all people, places, and events have been fictionalized or are purely fiction; historical fiction is somewhat rooted in real events. Many thanks to the multitude of authors, researchers, and helpful docents who put forth theories, histories and legends surrounding these times and events.

Thanks to:

Glencoe Visitor Centre, the National Trust for Scotland, and the National Trust for Scotland Foundation USA for educational exhibits and for protecting the natural glory of Glencoe as well as many other sites in Scotland; Historic Scotland for helping preserve the culture and castles of Scotland including many ruins; Kylie and Paul at the Falconry at Dalhousie Castle, Bonnyrigg, Scotland for their fabulous educational programs and patience in answering questions.

Special thanks to:

The members of the writing groups and other writing friends who graciously took me under their talented wings and from whom I continue to learn a great deal. Special thanks to Gwen, Gwen, Molly, Trish, Cathy, Sally, Ruth, Kay, Catherine, Cathy, Joyce, Mrs. Freeman and Dr. Wonz.

My nieces and nephews Sarah, Brian, Clara, Julia, Owen, Eliza, and Emily as well as Paige, Samantha Reese, and Cameron for reminding us how important it is, every once in a while, to be in awe.

My siblings for your patience and love.

Mom and Dad Macreery for your enthusiasm and encouragement.

Mom and Daddy for teaching me to love reading and history and for asking me to stretch myself.

Team Steve for an unforgettable adventure!

Most especially to my amazing husband, Bo, for his daily doses of encouragement, his courageous way of looking at life, his belief in this project and his faith in us. Leave nothing on the table.